Dana was sitting in class the next morning, listening to a boring lecture, when Bobby suddenly appeared in the doorway.

"Can I help you, Mr. Harrod?" the teacher asked.

"I have to talk to Dana Tafoya. It's an emergency."

Bobby looked pale and frantic. Dana grew alarmed.

"I have a pass," Bobby said, waving a piece of paper. "Please."

The teacher nodded and Dana scooted out the door. The hall was empty. "I'm on my way to the hospital." Bobby's eyes looked wild.

"What's wrong?" Dana's heart hammered and her mouth went dry.

"It's Steve," Bobby said, a tremor in his voice.

Lurlene McDaniel

How Do I Love Thee

Three Stories

Published by
Dell Laurel-Leaf
an imprint of
Random House Children's Books
a division of Random House, Inc.
New York

Visit us on the Web! www.randomhouse.com/teens
Educators and librarians, for a variety of teaching tools, visit us at
www.randomhouse.com/teachers

ISBN: 0-553-57107-9

RL: 5.4, ages 012 and up

Printed in the United States of America

A Bantam Book/December 2002
First Laurel-Leaf Edition May 2004

10 9 8 7 6 5
OPM

Thanks to all my wonderful readers

"Place me like a seal over your heart . . . for love is as strong as death. . . . It burns like blazing fire, like a mighty flame. Many waters cannot quench love; rivers cannot wash it away."

SONG OF SOLOMON 8:6–7

(NEW INTERNATIONAL VERSION)

Contents

Prologue

Over a hundred years ago, Elizabeth Barrett Browning wrote this sonnet for the man she loved:

HOW DO I LOVE THEE

How do I love thee? Let me count the ways.
I love thee to the depth and breadth and height
My soul can reach, when feeling out of sight
For the ends of Being and ideal Grace.
I love thee to the level of everyday's
Most quiet need, by sun and candle-light.
I love thee freely, as men strive for Right;
I love thee purely, as they turn from Praise.
I love thee with the passion put to use
In my old griefs, and with my childhood's faith.
I love thee with a love I seemed to lose
With my lost saints,—I love thee with the breath,
Smiles, tears, of all my life!—and, if God choose,
I shall but love thee better after death.

Love is not limited by time or space or age. It is the highest expression of human emotion.

When it is given purely, without expectation of return, and accepted freely, without parameters and conditions, it is a gift unto itself. Read, now, three stories of star-crossed lovers who experience love with amazing, life-changing depth. For one, a journey into love; for another, a rekindling of an old love; for the third, a sharing of noble, sacrificial love . . . for *all*, the discovery that true love transcends the self and makes a person the better for having touched it. Each person must learn that nothing can break love's bond, not even the face of death, and that this is one treasure that makes life beautiful.

BOOK ONE

Night Vision

One

The girl danced alone in the moonlight. Brett Noland stood behind a tree watching her, mesmerized. His watch dial glowed 1:00 A.M. When he'd left the cabin where his mother lay asleep to walk and think and figure out how he was going to accept all that had happened in the past month, he hadn't expected to see another living soul. Then he'd rounded a curve in the trail and seen a girl with long, dark hair twirling, swirling, spinning in an open field under the light of the bright full moon.

She wore a long ballerina skirt and held a filmy scarf that fluttered behind her like gossamer wings. There was no music that Brett could hear, only the sound of her graceful leaps in the tall grass. He wasn't sure if he should go back the way he came or wait until she left. The last thing he wanted was for her to catch him. It wasn't right to spy on people, but for the moment he felt glued to the ground.

She ran across the field, jumping and turning in the air like a gazelle. She slipped into the shadows of some trees. Brett held his breath, waiting for her to emerge into the field. She did not. He blinked, listened to the sound of the blood rushing in his ears. Where was she? She had seemed to disappear into thin air. Brett exhaled slowly and, feeling shaken, wondered if she had been there in the first place.

Maybe he'd imagined her. He'd felt stressed and hassled lately. So maybe the girl had only been a figment of an overactive imagination. The idea depressed him. On top of everything else, now he might be going nuts.

"Why are you spying on me?"

Her voice came from behind him, startling Brett so badly that he yelped. Whipping around, he saw her standing in the center of the trail, blocking his escape. "I—I wasn't spying," he said, his voice raspy, his heart pounding. "I was walking. I saw you. I didn't mean for you to see me."

"Then you shouldn't wear watches with glow-in-the-dark dials." She gestured to his wrist.

He covered the watch self-consciously, feeling foolish, and turned to face her more fully. "You do this often?" he asked, trying to regain his composure. "Dance under the moon?"

"Are you a reporter?"

"No . . . I'm Brett Noland. Who are you?"

She studied him, tipping her head to one side. Moonlight flecked her hair. "Shayla," she said.

She stepped forward, and he saw that she was tall, almost as tall as he was, which, according to his mother, was shorter than his father had been. When he'd had a father. "I just moved here," Brett blurted out when Shayla brushed past him to return to the open field.

"I didn't think you looked like a regular."

"What do regulars look like?" He followed her, suddenly not wanting to be alone. The girl intrigued him.

"Where are you from?" she asked.

"Key West, Florida."

She stopped. "Did you live near the sea?"

"Key West is almost surrounded by the sea, so yeah, I lived near it."

"Is it beautiful in the sunlight?"

Brett thought it a very odd question but decided to humor her. "Well, yes. But why—"

"Different from the sea up here, isn't it?"

"Everything's different up here, including the sea," he said bitterly. He and his mother had moved to the coastal town of Harden, Massachusetts, two weeks before. She'd taken a new job with a small seafood manufacturing plant, telling Brett it was time for a change, and no amount of begging her not to move had changed her mind. She kept telling him it was a big promotion, more money, a better opportunity. "And we'll be living closer to Boston Children's Hospital than we do to Miami Children's Hospital," she'd added, as if that would justify totally uprooting his life.

Brett hated his new location, a backwater town that squatted between the hills and woods to the west and the craggy shoreline of the ocean to the east. Industry consisted of fisheries that stunk of salt brine and fish processing. One of those fisheries had hired his mother to manage the office and product shipments. In the Keys, the ocean was pale green, warm and spiked with the smells of exotic flowers and tropical breezes. Here the coast was lined with rocks, not soft white sand. It was harsh, wild, unfriendly.

"You don't sound too happy to be here," Shayla said.

"I wanted to stay in Key West. I'll be a senior, and I wanted to finish school with my friends, but Mom took a new job, and I lost out."

"Tough break."

"You live here?"

"All my life."

"So what's school like?"

"I don't go to school."

Her answer caught him off guard. "Are you homeschooled?"

"Satellite-schooled."

"What's that?"

"I go to school on the Internet. And sometimes a homebound teacher comes over and spends time with me."

He was taken aback. Homebound teachers

only came to help sick kids. He knew that for a fact. Shayla looked normal, better than normal. "Do you live around here?"

"Beyond the woods. How about you?"

"Mom's renting a cabin." He motioned behind him, feeling awkward. Shayla wasn't forthcoming with information, and Brett didn't have much experience with girls. He was usually shy around them, perplexed and mystified by their capricious natures.

Shayla held the chiffon scarf across her eyes and peered up at the moon. "Pretty, isn't it?"

"Yes," he said, meaning both the moon and her. Now that he was closer, he saw that she really was pretty. Her hair fell straight and sleek almost to her waist. Her eyes were almond shaped and in the pale light looked like clear glass. He wondered what color they might be. "Did you sneak out to meet someone?"

"Did you?"

"Do you ever answer a question straight out?"

She laughed, and he thought that made her even prettier. "So tell me, Brett Noland, what did you think when you saw me dancing in the moonlight? Did you think I was crazy?"

"Are you?" Two could play her game of double questions.

"No." She threw the scarf into the air, and they both watched it flutter downward. "To both questions," she said. "I'm not crazy and I'm not meeting anyone."

"You just like to run around in the moonlight?"

"Yes."

He wanted to put her on the defensive. "I know—you're Titania."

"The fairy queen from *Midsummer Night's Dream*? Is that who you think I am?"

He was shocked that she had instantly known the character from Shakespeare's play. He read constantly, especially the classics, but knew few his age who did the same. "A druid then," he said.

"I don't worship trees," Shayla said with a toss of her head.

"You're a sprite."

"I'm too tall for a pixie."

"A ghost?"

"Some think so."

A shiver shot up his spine. This experience was turning surreal.

"Are you out of guesses?" she asked, making him feel undereducated, as if he'd forgotten some major category.

"I'm thinking," he said, racking his brain for another class of mythical beings who showed up only at night. He snapped his fingers. "Werewolves! No, wait—you don't have enough body hair to be a werewolf."

Again she laughed. "I think only men can be werewolves."

"You're right." He searched his memory, warming to the game they were playing. "Ah . . . I know, vampires come out at night. Are you a vampire?"

She looked straight at him and he felt his heart race crazily. The moon glowed along her hair, lit her face. Her skin was the color of sand, her eyes luminous, hypnotic pools. "Yes," she said. "I am."

TWO

❧

The hair on Brett's neck prickled. He waited for Shayla to laugh, or say "Just kidding," but she did not. His logic kicked in—perhaps she'd said what she did for shock value, using it as just another way to mystify him. He said, "All right, so you're a vampire. Does that mean I'm in trouble? Are you going to bite my neck and turn me into a vampire too?"

"Being a vampire isn't always about blood," Shayla said. "Vampires have other traits as well."

Brett was getting irritated. Why were girls so oblique? Why couldn't they say what they meant? "And those traits would be—?" He waited for her to fill in the blank.

"Since you seem to know so much about mythology and fairy tales, you tell me."

He told himself he should walk away, that Shayla was a nutcase. But he knew he wouldn't. In truth, this was the first interesting thing that had happened to him since his mother had dragged him to Massachusetts. He did say, "This is getting old, Shayla."

"So you don't know?" she asked, egging him on.

"Vampires are repelled by garlic," he said in a rush, rising to her challenge. "And by the Christian cross. They have a crypt that they return to every morning. Is that it? You sleep in a coffin?"

She clapped her hands gleefully, charming him all over again. "All that's true. Except that I wear this." She lifted a silver chain from beneath the neckline of her clothing, and moonlight glimmered off the surface of an ornate cross. "And I love garlic," she added, then looked up at him expectantly.

"So it's the crypt thing then, huh? You sleep in a crypt by day and only come out at night.

So, how is that . . . sleeping in such a small space, I mean?"

"That's a misconception. Crypts can be very large. They aren't always the size of a coffin. Sometimes they're the size of a mansion."

"What's *that* supposed to mean?"

She shook her head, as if she were dealing with a dolt. "Brett, Brett . . . I thought you were going to be smart. You still haven't figured it out, have you?"

He gritted his teeth. "It's two in the morning. I'm sharper in the daytime."

"Daylight, yes. Now you have it."

He felt oddly rewarded, as if she'd patted him on the head.

She turned to walk away.

He tagged after her. "Wait. I—um—I'm still thinking." He caught up with her in the middle of the field, where the moon had turned the world chalky white and a breeze made the tall grass whisper. "If a vampire is caught out in the sunlight, he burns. Worse, he can burst into flame and incinerate." Brett snapped his fingers. "Spontaneous combustion!" He grinned, feeling pleased with himself. "Is that the reason you're a vampire? You burn up in the sun?"

Her face was expressionless, her eyes clear as water. She trailed the scarf across his forearm, making his skin shiver, then leaned forward and kissed him lightly on the mouth. "Goodbye, Brett Noland."

Before he could move, she had turned and sprinted into a stand of trees. "Wait!" he yelled. Night birds fluttered in the tree branches with the unexpected sound. A rabbit darted from the edge of the field. Clumsily, Brett tried to follow, but by the time he'd made it to the trees, there was no sign of her. All that remained was the sweet, lingering scent of her fragrance in the shadows where the moonlight didn't reach.

Brett returned to the clearing in the woods every night for a week, but Shayla did not reappear. He waited for up to an hour each night, even fell asleep propped against a tree one night, only to wake shivering because the temperature had dropped.

He sat at the kitchen table on Saturday, hunched over his third bowl of cereal, yawning and struggling to keep his eyes open. Suddenly, his mother slapped the tabletop, startling him awake.

"What's wrong with you, Brett? You're like a zombie these days. Are you feeling okay, because if you're not—"

If you only knew, Mom, he thought. "I feel fine." He leaned back over the bowl.

"You're really making me angry, Brett."

"What did *I* do?"

"Nothing, Brett. Which is precisely the problem. You're doing *nothing*!"

"Ah, geez, Mom, get off my case." He pushed his chair back so that it balanced on the back legs.

"Don't use that tone of voice with me. And sit down properly." She started clearing the table. "How long are you going to keep punishing me for moving up here?" She didn't wait for his answer. "I want a shot at a better life, Brett, and this move was for both our sakes. You want to go to college next year. Just how did you think I was going to afford that, making the kind of money I was making in Key West?"

"I didn't ask you to send me to college.

Maybe I don't even want to go to college. I'm not out of high school yet."

"You have to plan for the things you want, Brett. It's been you and me for a long time, and so far we've gotten on pretty well."

Brett rolled his eyes. "Thirteen years, yeah, Mom, I can count. And you've told me enough."

"Then get with the program! You still have to go to the high school and register, and we have to check in at Boston Children's Hospital. I'll handle the hospital appointment because I'll have to take off work. Can you call and make the appointment to register with the school? You can schedule it for my lunch hour." He didn't respond. "Don't you want to see where you'll be going to school in September?"

"I can hardly contain myself."

She spun him around, hovered over him. He saw fire in her eyes. "Listen to me, Brett. I love you, but you're going to have to meet me halfway. I can't give my full concentration to my job if I'm worried about you all the time."

"What do you want me to do, Mom?" He felt guilty because, looking into her face, he saw that she was tired and stressed. "I have nothing to do all day. No friends, no nothing."

She straightened. "Get a job. Believe me, that will really pass the time."

"No car."

"You can drop me at work Monday morning and keep the car all day."

Her offer surprised him. She usually wasn't so generous with their only car because she thought he drove around aimlessly and used too much gas—". . . and gas isn't cheap."

"You'd let me do that?"

"If you'll promise to be responsible. And if you'll promise to go by the school and take care of registering before it completely shuts down for the summer."

After leaving his mother at work on Monday, Brett drove slowly along the coastal highway. A thick gray fog hung over the road, and he wanted to be careful. He didn't want an accident to foul up his driving privileges, or his mother's trust in him. Wheels meant freedom.

He turned on the radio, found a station that didn't play corny oldies, his mother's favorites, and considered how to best spend the day. He didn't have to pick up his mother until five. He glanced out the side window and saw a road that had been cut through solid granite. It led to a house perched at the top of a jutting cliff. The house, built of dark brown clapboard, had a turret and a walkway with a banister across the roof. The great house hovered far above the fog, but despite the gloom, he saw no lights in the windows. The place looked abandoned.

"Who'd want to live in a house like that?" he asked aloud. No . . . not a house—a mansion. Brett sat straighter. What had Shayla said to him? *A crypt the size of a mansion!* "Yes," he yelped. He was going to find the mysterious Shayla whether she wanted him to or not.

Three

Deciding he'd better take care of business first, Brett found his way to the high school, an old brick building covered on two sides with ivy. He parked and went inside. The halls were painted a pale, institutional shade of green and smelled of chalk dust and floor wax. The old wooden floor creaked, and banks of battered lockers ran the length of the walls. He wasn't impressed, especially since his high school in the Keys had been newly built and outfitted with the latest equipment. He found the main office, talked to a secretary about transferring his records up from Florida, filled out paperwork, and was told he'd receive room assignments in late August. He was given a packet and was leaving the office when a guy about his age said, "Hey, man. You're new, huh?"

Brett turned and faced a short, muscular kid with bleached blond hair, an ear stud, and a big grin. "Sure am," Brett said, liking the guy at once.

"I'm Douglas Tredmont, but everyone calls me Dooley. I wasn't eavesdropping, but I did hear you registering. So you're from Key West? Long way from here."

"Tell me about it."

"I understand culture shock; I moved here from Chicago three years ago."

In the hall, Brett paused. "You like it?"

Dooley shrugged. "About as much as dental surgery—at first, anyway. I'm okay with it now."

"I don't think I'll ever be okay with it. I'm a senior. How about you?"

"Same. That is if I pass algebra during the summer session. Which is why I'm here to-day." Dooley pointed down the hall. "I'd give you a tour, but I'd be late to class."

"I'll tour it when I have to, but thanks for the offer."

"Look, if you really get bored, come to Bud's Pizza Palace on State Street any night. It's where most of us hang. Us cool ones, that is," he added with a wink. "Bud's got a few pool tables, and there's always a game going."

Pleased by the invitation, Brett grinned. "I was wondering what people did for fun around here. Thanks, I'll check it out."

"I'll look for you."

Brett started to walk off, stopped, and asked, "Say, you must know your way around the town. Can you tell me who lives in that creepy house up on the bluff when you're driving along the coast highway?"

Dooley thought for a moment. "You must mean the old Brighton house—home of the Ghost Girl."

Brett's pulse quickened. "A *ghost* lives there?"

"Not a real ghost, but a girl who only comes out at night. They say she's allergic to the sun. I've heard plenty of talk about her."

"I never heard of being allergic to the sun."

"Me either, but it must be pretty serious because she never comes to school. Only the kids who've lived here since they were babies have ever seen her, and that was in elementary school. I saw her once walking around on some little balcony on the roof of her house in the moonlight. Weird, huh?"

A tingle shot up Brett's spine. "Sounds weird to me."

The bell rang. Dooley headed up the hall. "Talk to you later, man. Remember, Bud's Pizza Palace. Come meet the gang."

Brett left the school, certain he'd found the mysterious Shayla but uncertain what to do about it. He headed into town, parked, and hit a few of the businesses to fill out job applications. Most of the summer work available was at the docks and harbor, but that wasn't where he wanted to be.

A fast-food place offered him a job on the spot. "You'll have to work the evening shift," the manager told him. "I need someone from four till eleven, Tuesday through Saturday. You'll get forty minutes for a supper break at six."

Brett almost turned it down, then realized

that evening work would allow him to keep the car all day. He could drop his mother at her job, then go home and sleep. And if he used his supper break, he could pick up his mother, take her home, and drive himself back to work so that she wouldn't have to pick him up so late. If he liked hanging at Bud's with Dooley and his friends, he could meet them after work, while his mother slept. Brett told the manager he'd take the job.

Brett drove home, pleased with his progress. His mother had no need to crab at him now. He'd registered for school and gotten a job. In the process, he'd touched base with a potential friend and found out about Shayla. Whether she was a ghost or a vampire didn't matter to him. He wanted to get to know her because there was something about her that wouldn't let him go.

His mother wasn't crazy about Brett having the car almost full time, but she said they could try the schedule for a while and see if it worked. She added, "I made an appointment for you with a Dr. Packtor at Children's Hospital a week from Thursday, so you'll have to make arrangements with your new boss to get off."

Brett complained, knowing that the trip into Boston would eat up an entire day.

"It's not up for negotiation," his mother said.

"My doctor checked me before we left Florida. I'm fine."

"You need a specialist to keep an eye on you. Besides, I want a medical team in place . . . just in case."

"You mean just in case it comes back?" Brett grumbled. "It's been five years, Mom."

"You're going. That's final," she told him.

"We don't have to broadcast it all over town, do we? I mean, if I'm lucky enough to make friends here, they don't all have to know I've had leukemia, do they?"

"No." She rubbed the back of her neck wearily. "The administration at the new school needs to know, but you don't have to tell any-one else."

"They'll treat me like a freak, you know."

"I can't understand why anybody would treat you like an outcast just because you had a horrible disease when you were ten."

"But they do," he said. "Take it from me."

She would never understand what it had

been like for him. First the mysterious bruises on his body, fatigue, and pain in his bones. Then the diagnosis and two hellish years of treatment with a relapse at age twelve. He'd practically lived at the children's hospital in Miami, where he'd been poked and jabbed and filled with toxic chemotherapy that made him so sick he couldn't even get out of bed without throwing up. He'd lost his hair, about a third of his body weight, and almost all of his friends. And when remission finally came, he still wasn't home free. There had been monthly trips to the hospital, then semiannual visits, now annual ones for blood work and the possibility of painful bone marrow aspirations. But the doctors had told him that if he got past the magic five-year mark there was a good chance he'd beaten the odds. At seventeen, he thought of himself as cured. It was his mother who constantly worried about him relapsing.

"I almost lost you, Brett. A trip to Boston to meet with a new doctor will give me peace of mind." Tears welled in her eyes, making him feel instant guilt for giving her a hard time. She'd always been there for him. Before leukemia, during leukemia when his father had cut out, after leukemia when it had been just the two of them.

He put his arm around her shoulders. "Turn off the waterworks, Mom," he said kindly. "We'll go see this new doctor, and I won't go all postal on you. Maybe we can check out Boston while we're there. Home of the Red Sox, you know."

She sniffed and wiped her cheek. "Not to mention the Boston Tea Party and the start of the Revolutionary War."

"Did that happen in Boston? Who knew?" he joked, and was rewarded by her smile.

Brett drove home from work along the coastal highway so that he could pass the Brighton house. He'd had his job barely a week before he was rewarded by the sight of a lone figure on the rooftop balcony. He pulled over to the side of the road, turned off his headlights, and got out of the car. He saw the girl quite clearly etched against the summer sky, lit by a waning moon. Under his breath, he said, "Hello, Shayla. I think it's time we meet again."

Four

Brett crossed the deserted highway and walked up the steep side road that led to the yard and driveway of the old house. He was panting by the time he got to the top. Except for a lone candle that glowed by a back door next to the turret, the house was pitch-black. He saw a narrow outside spiral staircase that wound up the turret and he started toward it.

This is stupid, he told himself, *not to mention risky. What if there's an alarm? Or a vicious dog?* But he'd gone too far to stop now. He made his way up the winding stairway, careful to be as quiet as possible. By the time he reached the top, he was soaked with perspiration. He remained on a rung of the ladder just below the landing and peered onto the narrow balcony.

Shayla was leaning on the rail, staring at the ocean. He also saw a stool and a book, although he couldn't figure out how she read in the dark. With his heart hammering, Brett pulled himself onto the narrow walkway. "Hello," he said. "Are you planning to fly down, like a vampire bat?"

She started and cried out.

"Don't be scared. It's me," he said hurriedly. "Brett Noland, from the woods."

Even in the scant light he could tell she wasn't pleased to see him. "You're trespassing."

"I know, but I chanced it anyway because I wanted to see you again. I went out to the woods for a while, but you never came back."

"You did?" She looked surprised.

"You got to me, Shayla. I've never met a girl with such a great pickup line." He tried humor. "I mean, most girls only have bad hair days—hardly a topic for deep conversations."

"How many girls do you know?"

He grinned. She was quick. "Actually, you're the only girl I've met since I moved here, and you won't even talk to me, so that makes none."

She walked to the stool, picked up the book, and held it across her chest like a shield. "But you've heard something about me, haven't you?"

"Yes, on the day I registered for school." He didn't want to lie to her.

"So you're here to see the Ghost Girl. Don't look surprised. I know what they call me. What else did they tell you?"

"They said you were allergic to the sun."

She neither confirmed nor denied the information.

He tried again. "I work nights. I was on my way home, and I saw you up here, so I came up to talk."

She kept looking at him, as if sizing him up.

He wanted her to relax and trust him. He peered over the side of the balcony, at the jagged rocks far below. "Is this the widow's walk?"

"Yes," she said.

He'd read enough to know that during the whaling days, when ships went out for months at a time, wives and girlfriends went up to the rooftop balconies to watch for a ship's return. If it came with its flag flying at half-mast, it meant men had died. One of his favorite books was *Moby Dick*, so he knew how dangerous harpooning whales could be. "This house must be really old," he said. "And I'll bet it knew plenty of widows."

"My grandfather bought it from a ninety-three-year-old widow who lost her husband at sea. She became a recluse, and after she died people could see her ghost walking up here at night."

"Have you seen her ghost?"

"No. But ghosts like to keep to themselves."

"Is that what you'd like? To be by yourself?"

"I usually am."

"I'd like to come see you again."

"Why? So you can talk about me to people at school?"

"I'm not going to tell anyone about us if that's what you want."

"Us . . ." She said the word slowly, as if tasting it. "I've never been an 'us.' "

He felt her loneliness as if it were a living thing and realized why she was so defensive.

No one could hurt you if you didn't let anyone get close to you. "Look, I'm going to write down my phone number. Call me if you want me to come back. Otherwise, I won't bother you." He patted his pockets for a pen but couldn't find one.

She watched, then finally pulled one out from under the book she was clutching. He began a new search for something to write on, failed, and gave her a helpless shrug. She smiled slightly, offered the book. He noted that it was *Sonnets from the Portuguese* by Elizabeth Barrett Browning. He scribbled his phone number on the inside cover and handed it back. "Call me, Shayla. Please."

She gave him a lingering look, then turned and stepped through a window that was also a door, disappearing into the darkness of the great house. He stood alone on the widow's walk, missing her, imagining a storm-tossed sea and generations of sailors who had never returned, now watched over by a girl who could not walk in the sun.

Brett and his mother drove to Boston Children's Hospital in the rain. The hospital was enormous, encompassing several blocks along the river. A playground for younger children stood sodden in the downpour. Indoors, the building housed an atrium filled with gray light from massive windows and a skylight. They rode up to the oncology floor, where Brett met a round of doctors, assistants, social workers, and technicians. His final stop was with Dr. Leonard Packtor, who looked to be in his forties and was a specialist in blood cancers of adolescents.

"What do you think of the place?" Dr. Packtor asked.

"It's big."

The doctor laughed. "Listen, we've gotten your records, which I've gone over. It seems you received excellent treatment and that the chemo protocols did the trick. There was no sign of cancer in your last checkup."

Brett gave his mother a "see-I-told-you" look. Sometimes he wondered if she hated to let go of his illness because it meant letting go of him. It made no sense to him that she'd think that way, but nevertheless, it was often the way she acted.

"I only want Brett in your system," his mother said. "Just in case."

"He's in our system," the doctor said.

"This thing's behind me, isn't it, Doc?" Brett asked.

"Can't say for sure. You know, years ago, leukemia was a certain death sentence. Now we have patients experiencing ten- and fifteen-year remissions."

"So I'm not cured?" Brett felt his heart squeeze.

"I never use the word 'cured' when talking about cancer. That's why you come every year for a checkup. You're looking good, and we'll stay on top of it. If you experience any unusual symptoms, call me."

Brett disliked the lack of optimism in the doctor's tone. Why couldn't he just say, "You're fine and cancer will never come your way again"? It would be much kinder.

Brett stood. "Are we finished?"

"Unless you have questions, yes."

Brett saw several on his mother's face and was grateful when she didn't ask them. She was always scared for his health. "I have one," he said. "But it's not about leukemia. This hospital treats all kinds of diseases, doesn't it?"

"Kids with diseases—no matter how rare—are our specialty. What do you want to know about?"

"A disease that a kid's born with that makes them allergic to the sun."

Dr. Packtor looked thoughtful. "You mean a sun rash?"

"No. Getting burned, burned really bad, if the sun even touches their skin."

His mother grimaced.

"Perhaps you mean *xeroderma pigmentosum*, or XP for short. We call them Children of the Moon."

Five

A child of the moon—yes, that described Shayla perfectly. "Can you tell me about XP?" Brett asked.

"It's a genetic disorder," Dr. Packtor said. "Victims' DNA repair mechanisms don't work properly, making them severely sensitive to ultraviolet radiation."

"Sunlight," Brett said.

"Actually any kind of UV light, but sunlight especially. There's no cure for XP, but fortunately, it's rare—maybe only a thousand cases worldwide. Kids from all over the Northeast come here for treatment."

"What happens to people with XP?"

"Every time they are exposed to UV light, their DNA is irreversibly damaged. They're very susceptible to eye and skin cancers, melanoma being the worst of the skin variety. Even normal people can get melanomas. That's why we tell people not to get sunburned and to use sunscreen faithfully." He shrugged. "But they don't listen."

"So a kid with XP can't ever get well?" Brett's heart sank.

"No, but some cases are worse than others. Many XP victims also have severe handicaps, such as blindness, deafness, even mental retardation. Most victims die young. It's imperative that they limit sun exposure, which means turning themselves into night people. It's a hard life, especially when they're kids. But there is a kids' camp. Every year Camp Sundown is held in July in upstate New York for three weeks. The kids sleep all day, play all night."

"But isn't there research going on to help these children?" This came from Brett's mother, who sounded aghast.

"There's always research, but because so

few people have it, it's not a high priority. Sad but true."

"So if Brett had had XP instead of leukemia, then he wouldn't have had *any* possibility of getting well?"

"True," said Dr. Packtor.

"Sucky," Brett said.

In the car, driving home, Brett's mother asked, "Why did you ask about XP? Do you know someone with it?"

"I've heard talk at the burger joint about an XP girl who lives in our town," Brett said, unwilling to talk about Shayla or endure endless questions from his mother about how they met and so on.

"I can't imagine raising a child with such a disorder. Her parents must go to extraordinary lengths to cope."

"It's no piece of cake for her either," Brett declared.

"I'm sure that's true, but can you imagine what her parents' lives must be like? They still have to hold down jobs and live in the daytime world, yet their child can't. What a heartache. I'm so glad XP isn't your problem."

"At least her parents can come and go as they please," he said. "They aren't pinned under glass where everybody who's normal can stare at them and make them feel like an outcast."

His mother gave him a quizzical look. "What's gotten into you? All I said was I felt sorry for her parents."

"And I feel sorrier for her," Brett fired back. "Her parents can walk out the door. She can't."

The veiled reference to his father made his mother withdraw. Instantly he felt bad about firing the shot. Brett's diagnosis had contributed to his father's leaving. He hadn't been able to handle having a sick son who could die suddenly. Just one more reason why Brett wanted to be cured—it was an act of defiance, proof to his father, who never saw them anymore, that leaving had been an act of cowardice.

When Brett got off work on Friday night, he hunted down Bud's Pizza Palace.

"Hey, Brett!" Dooley called out as soon as

Brett walked in the door. "Where have you been? I've been telling the gang about you, but you never showed up. We were all beginning to think I was hallucinating."

"Been busy," Brett said. "But I've got a rhythm now, and so here I am."

"Let me introduce you around." Dooley pointed toward a cluster of teens, gave them names that included Hal, Roberta, Sandy, BJ, Toby, Susan, Kyle, and Blake.

Brett tried to keep up, but the faces sort of blurred together, and he wasn't sure he could put the right name with the right face. "Hi," he said self-consciously.

"You shoot pool?" Dooley asked.

"Some." In truth, Brett was a good pool player. He'd spent many hours perfecting his game when he was recovering from the devastation of leukemia treatments, too sick to go to school. He had played against himself and, when he was well enough, against his next-door neighbor, an elderly man who taught him much about the game. Brett liked pool better than computer games. He liked the geometry of it.

Dooley racked the balls. Brett was nervous, so it took him a while to hit his stride, but he was soon being looked at with respect by Dooley and his friends.

"Where did you learn to play like that?" BJ asked.

"I just picked it up over time."

"Seems to me like you spent a lot of time at it," Susan said. She was one of the better players in the group. "Seems to me you suckered us."

"Hey, stop dissing my man," Dooley said. "They're just jealous," he added to Brett.

"No need to be," Brett said, pleased that he had a skill that impressed the kids he'd be going to school with in the fall. "It's only a game."

"I could use a few lessons," Sandy said, sidling up to him.

The others made kissy sounds. Brett felt his face turn red. It wasn't often a girl noticed him, much less hit on him. "I'm working a lot," he said lamely.

Sandy leaned toward him. "Well, if you ever find yourself with time on your hands, give me a call."

More teasing from the others, which Sandy ignored and Brett laughed off.

Eventually Brett told them he had to leave. They invited him to come again, which he promised to do, but all the way home he wondered how they would feel if they knew he'd once had cancer. Probably not nearly so friendly. People were afraid of cancer, and kids were downright cruel about it. He'd never forget the sense of ostracism he'd felt in middle school.

When he arrived home, his mother had gone to bed. A lamp burned in the living room, and a note was stuck on the refrigerator with a magnet. It read:

Brett,

Some girl named Shayla called around 11. I'm glad you're making friends, but can you please tell them to call earlier? Eleven at night is simply too late to hear the phone ring. I thought it was you and that something bad had happened.

Brett's heartbeat accelerated. Shayla called! He wanted to talk to her before she changed her mind about talking to him. He eased out the door, returned to the car, slipped it into neutral, and pushed it away from the cabin driveway. He didn't start the engine or turn on the headlights until he'd nosed onto the road, heading toward Shayla's house.

Six

~

Brett drove up to Shayla's house, cut the engine, then sat wondering how he was going to get hold of her. It was after midnight. Surely her family was asleep. He saw a candle flickering on the back porch, so he took a chance and rapped lightly on the screen.

She appeared out of the darkness, startling him. "I—um, heard that you called."

"I was going to ask you to come over."

"I know it's late—"

"Maybe for you, but I've only been up for a few hours."

Her days were his nights, he reminded himself.

"I know you work," she said. "If tonight's not good for you—"

"Tonight's fine," he said hastily, not wanting to miss his opportunity. She could change her mind by tomorrow. "I can sleep in because my shift doesn't start until four o'clock." He jingled the car keys in his pocket nervously. Finally, he confessed, "Look, Shayla, I know about your having XP."

She remained quiet for so long that he was afraid she was going to tell him to go away. Instead, she asked, "And you came anyway?"

"Why wouldn't I?"

She opened the screen door. "Follow me." She picked up the candle and took him down a flight of stairs.

"Your room's in the basement?"

"Underground is the safest place for me. Only two tiny windows that Dad painted black."

At the foot of the stairs, she opened a door, and he saw a huge room that glowed with lit candles and low-wattage lightbulbs. The room reminded him of an apartment, with a living area, a dining area, and kitchen. There was a brick fireplace in one wall, and large pieces of comfortable furniture were arranged cozily to face it. Another wall was covered by a massive array of electronic equipment—a TV, VCR, DVD and CD players, stacks of CDs, and shelves of videotapes. Bookshelves crammed with books lined two other walls, and a long desk held three computers with screens aglow, a fax machine, and a small scanner. A cat jumped off the sofa and sauntered over to rub against Shayla's leg and check out Brett.

"Welcome to my crypt," she said.

"Is all this yours?" He could hardly believe his eyes.

"I come alive at night, remember? I need something to do while the rest of the world sleeps." She started around the room, pointing to things as she went. "That door leads to my bedroom and bathroom. In there is a food pantry so that I don't have to go upstairs in the daytime for anything. This computer is for schoolwork, this one for games, this one I only use to surf the Net and keep up with my friends, others like me. The screens are specially coated for my protection. The lamps have special bulbs that emit lower levels of UV light. The candles are for atmosphere and because I love candlelight. Any questions?"

He was awed by the complexity of her setup, by the extreme precautions taken to protect her. "Not too shabby," he said, hoping he didn't sound like a dweeb.

She sat on the sofa and patted the cushion next to her. He sat beside her. "My parents are good people. They've done everything they can to make my life as normal as possible. I used to get mad at them because they wouldn't let me do anything they thought might hurt me. Actually, now that I'm older, I feel sorry for them. They never asked to have an XP child. But because they did, they knew they carried the genes for it and so they never had another one. They feel responsible for bringing me into the world, and now that I'm here, they feel responsible for keeping me safe."

"How did they find out you had XP?" Now that she was willing to talk to him about her disorder, he wanted to hear everything.

"When I was a baby, Mom took me outside and sat me on a blanket under a tree while she did some gardening. I started to scream bloody murder. She ran over and discovered that I was covered with huge red welts and blisters. She rushed me to the emergency room, and the doctor said I had third-degree burns on my arms and face. He believed my mother had deliberately burned me, that I was abused."

"But it was the sunlight, wasn't it?"

Shayla nodded. "Even fluorescent lights burned me. My parents had to completely reconfigure this house and make it lightproof. We started fixing up the basement for me when I was eight. It was much easier to live down here than upstairs."

"Didn't you ever go to regular school?"

"I tried in third grade. The school had to cover the windows and lower the lights whenever I came for the day. My mother had to toss a blanket over me so that I could ride in the car to even get there. I felt like a freak sitting in the backseat with a blanket over my head. In fourth and fifth grade, I came less often because kids started making fun of me. They called me Ghost Girl and Earthworm. By sixth grade, I stopped coming altogether. Teachers came here, and of course, there was the Web. No big deal."

It was a big deal. Brett recalled how he'd felt when he'd been called names. "And now?"

"Now I've moved ahead and left them in the dust." She offered a smile. "I've already completed a year of courses from Boston College on the Internet. College is more fun anyway, and a whole lot more challenging."

"I'm impressed. I can hardly keep up with high school."

"There's nothing to distract me, you know, like football games, or cliques of dopey girls talking about their boyfriends."

She'd left unsaid the things that were good about school, but he didn't argue. He asked, "Do you ever go out in the daytime?"

"Sometimes . . . when the sun's just gone down, or first thing in the morning. But I don't stay out long, and I have to rub on gobs of sunscreen." She went to the bookshelves, selected a videotape, and inserted it into the VCR. The TV screen lit up with a clip of the sun glowing like an enormous red ball over the plains of Africa. The scene shifted to images of a white-sand beach where people sunbathed and a pale green sea lapped the shoreline. Brett could almost feel the heat on his skin.

Shayla froze the tape on a shot of the sun burning white-hot in a blue sky. "Dirty pictures," she joked, making him laugh. "The sun fascinates me. I wish . . . I wish I could feel it without it hurting."

The longing in her voice unsettled him. He held out his arm, tanned from a lifetime of beach-going and skin diving in the Florida Keys. By comparison, her skin looked white as milk. "Your skin is beautiful," he said. "You should see some of the old guys in Florida who've spent too much time in the sun. They look like old leather saddles."

She ran her hand across his skin and made a tingling sensation race up his back. "Why are you being nice to me, Brett?"

"Because I like you."

"You're going back to the others to tell them all about meeting up with the Ghost Girl, aren't you? Please don't talk about me." She sounded so sad that it hurt his heart.

"I told you I wouldn't do that." He took a deep breath. "Shayla, I know what it feels like to be on the outside looking in."

"How could you? You're perfect."

His heart began to hammer. He wanted her to know he was more like her than she realized and that she was special to him. "Not perfect," he said, his long-held secret trembling in his mouth. "Once, I had leukemia."

Seven

~

Brett told Shayla of his bout with leukemia. He held her hand while he talked and when he paused or choked up, she squeezed his fingers as if to help him over the rough places in his memory. He'd never spoken so frankly to anyone before about his feelings, but in Shayla, he believed he'd found acceptance and understanding. When he was finished, he felt cleansed.

"I'm glad you made it," she told him, tears in her eyes.

He brushed them away. "I didn't tell you so you'd feel sorry for me. Pity's the last thing I want." He leaned forward, wanting to kiss her so much he ached.

Her eyes widened as she understood his intention. He saw her lips part, tremble. Suddenly one of her computers beeped, making both of them jump. "I've got mail," she explained with a nervous laugh.

Bad timing, he thought. The spell was broken.

She went to the desk and clicked the mouse. "I keep in touch with other XP kids and sometimes we message back and forth all night long."

He looked at the clock on the mantel over the fireplace, let out a shout, and jumped to his feet. "It's two A.M. I've got to get home."

"I'm sorry. I didn't mean for you to—"

He placed his fingertips over her mouth. "Cool it. I wanted to stay. Wild horses couldn't have dragged me away. Truth is, I want to come back. I want to know everything there is to know about you."

"I'm very boring," she said.

"Not to me." He kissed her forehead. "I'll call you tomorrow night as soon as I go home and check in with Mom. Then once she's asleep, I'm coming to see you." He stopped at the door and turned as a bold idea struck him. "Would your parents mind if we went out tomorrow night—you know, like on a date?"

She laughed. "I'm almost eighteen, and Mom and Dad don't hold me prisoner. I know the rules about how to take care of myself."

"Good. Then how about packing up some food? I'd like to take us on a picnic in the moonlight."

When Brett coasted into Shayla's driveway at midnight, she was ready to go. He set the basket she'd prepared in the backseat and drove off. "I've cased some places," he told her, "but the best place is that field where I first saw you dancing."

"You must have thought I was loony that night."

"I was too surprised at first to think much more than 'Wow, what a pretty girl.' "

"I never expected anyone to actually catch me out there. I saw you moving in the trees and almost ran away, but then decided to sneak around behind you and find out what you were doing in the woods so late at night."

"Well, I'm glad you did . . . even though I almost made a run for it when you told me you were a vampire." He bared his teeth and she laughed. "Why *did* you say that to me?"

"Because I'm a big fan of mythology and folktales. I grew up reading everything I could get my hands on about fairies, elves, vampires, and such. I honestly think that these kinds of stories are rooted in truth. One day I got to thinking about how people in medieval times would have reacted to a child born with XP."

"They would have probably drowned 'em," Brett said. He was a fan of history and knew that superstitions had generally been held as truth before the emergence of science.

"But think about it—a person put her child in the sun and suddenly the child started to 'burn.' It would have blown their medieval minds."

"And demanded an explanation," Brett added.

"Exactly. So storytellers started incorporating the fact about sunlight burning a person into the legend about the vampire because it couldn't be explained any other way."

"A legend Bram Stoker writes about in

Dracula." Brett grinned. "That's an interesting theory, Shayla."

"I wrote it up and it was published in a medical journal," she said, sounding pleased with Brett's approval.

"Now I'm *really* impressed," he said. "Way to go."

By now they were parked at the edge of the wooded area. Brett carried the basket and Shayla the blanket as they made their way to the field. The grass had been mowed, and now the field looked flat and gray in the light of the crescent moon. Brett spread the blanket under the stars. Shayla took candles from the basket and lit them. The twinkling light cast a rosy glow on her face. Brett was struck by her ethereal beauty and swallowed hard. He wished he had the courage to kiss her, but he didn't.

They ate the food she'd packed while night sounds of tree frogs and crickets surrounded them. "This is fun," she said, nibbling on a grape. "I've never been on a picnic before."

"You mean a picnic in the moonlight," he corrected.

"No, a picnic *ever.*"

He wasn't sure why her confession pleased

him so much, but it did. "There's plenty of things I'd like to do with you, Shayla."

She leaned toward him, her eyes shining in the flickering of the candles. "Tonight we did something I've never done before. Now it's your turn to do something with me you've never done before."

In Brett's mind, the list was endless, beginning with kissing her. "Such as?"

"Wait until tomorrow night and I'll show you."

Shayla was at the foot of the steep road leading up to her driveway when Brett arrived the next night. "Park here," she said, motioning to a spot next to her family's roadside mailbox. She was wearing a sweatshirt and handed one to him. "We're going across the street."

"The ocean's across the street," he said, taking her offered hand and jogging beside her over the deserted main road.

"Things aren't always what they seem," she whispered mysteriously.

On the far side of the road, seawater splashed against a jumble of rocks, in the midst of which stood a small boathouse. Inside there was a wooden dinghy, complete with oars and a small motor. "Yours?" he asked.

"Dad bought it for me when I was fifteen. I'd rather have a sailboat, but unless there's a gale, there's no wind at night." They stepped into the boat.

"I had one like this in the Keys. My friends and I used to take it out to the reef and skin dive."

"I use it to putter around offshore." She pulled the starter cord, and the outboard motor sputtered to life.

In minutes they were skimming across the glassy calm of a quiet sea. The night air was frigid on his face, and he was grateful for the sweatshirt. "You know where you're going?" he yelled above the roar of the motor.

"Don't you trust me?"

He gave her a thumbs-up, sat back, and enjoyed the ride. When they were far offshore and the lights along the highway and on the tip of the harbor looked like twinkling jewels, Shayla cut the engine. Brett heard waves lapping against the wooden sides of the boat before the water settled into calm again. Stars littered the night sky like white confetti. Shayla hunkered down next to him.

"Where are we?" he asked.

"We're inside a natural rock formation. You can't see the rocks because it's high tide."

"What if you hit a rock? Knock a hole in the boat?"

"Relax, I've been coming out here for years. I know my way around. When the tide goes out, it's like you're inside a bowl."

"There's no way out?"

"Not unless you're a seagull. But as soon as the tide comes back in, you float right out. Neat, huh?"

"Not as neat as you," he said. He reached for her, pulled her close, and felt the warmth of her body against his. "What do you do when you come out here?" he asked, pressing his mouth into her thick, dark hair which smelled like flowers.

"I *think*," she said, her voice trembling with emotion. "I think about having a regular life. I think about what I want to do with whatever time I have left to live."

Eight

Her answer startled him. Distracted by his feelings, he'd almost forgotten how different she was, how unique her life's course. Dr. Packtor had told him that XP victims die young. "H-how long do you have to live?"

"I don't know, but I've had two melanomas taken off in the past year. Sooner or later, no matter how careful I am, a melanoma will metastasize and spread. My best friend's dying. We used to go to Camp Sundown together— that's a special camp where kids with XP get together once a year and have fun."

"You aren't going this year?"

She shook her head. "I can't face it knowing Kimberly won't be there. She's too sick."

"Where is she?"

"Canada. We first met when we were both twelve. We burned up the Net with e-mail, met every year at camp. But now . . ." Shayla shrugged. "I can't even go see her."

His heart hurt for Shayla, for Kimberly, and for all the children who had this terrible disorder. "You've still got me," he ventured.

She pulled away and searched his face with her clear, pale eyes. "What happens when school starts? You won't have time for me then."

"No way. I'll work something out."

"I know you think that's true, but your life's in the daylight. You can't go to school all day, study, run around with your friends, and see me at night. You'll have to sleep sometime."

"I don't know how I'll do it either, but I will. Shayla, you've hidden yourself away too long. I've met some of the kids from this town, and they're pretty okay. Maybe it's time to get reacquainted with them."

"I can't."

"They're just kids like us."

"Not one bit like us. You've never had them call you names."

"That was years ago. Everybody grows up. A whole group of them meets at Bud's Pizza Palace. We shoot pool, have a good time. Come with me. You'll have fun, and they'll get to know you—the real you. They'll see how wonderful you are."

"Why are you asking me to do this?" She moved away from his side.

"Because I want to date you. I want to take you to football games and dances. You said you could do things at night if you're careful, and I want you to be with me as much as possible."

"Once school starts, you'll feel differently."

"Stop trying to change my mind." Brett was getting upset. "It's *you*, I want, Shayla. Why don't you believe me?"

"Don't you think I've wanted this all my life? To be normal . . . to have what other girls have?" Her eyes filled with tears, and he felt terrible. The last thing he wanted was to make her cry. "It isn't possible, Brett."

"Not true," he said, careful to not sound angry. "The only thing standing in your way is you. You're afraid. Believe me, I know all about being afraid. And I'm not talking about being afraid of dying. Sometimes living's much harder than dying. When Mom dragged me up here, I was scared to death. I hated her for making us move. But I met you. And I've made a few friends. And I have a job. And you know what? I'm happy."

"You're not a moon child," she said solemnly, and moved to the back of the boat. She started the motor and aimed the dinghy toward the shore.

Brett was glad of the noise of the motor because they couldn't talk. He'd said too much, gone too far. He could kick himself for pushing her. The kids he knew and liked had taunted and ridiculed her when she was younger because she'd been different. She'd made new friends with others who suffered from XP and who accepted her. She wasn't ready to enter his world, and he'd been stupid to try to push her.

She docked the boat in the boathouse. They crossed the road without speaking. At his car, she said, "It'll be better if we don't see each other for a while."

"Shayla, I'm sorry—"

"Please . . . I need some time."

He watched her bolt up the road toward the great dark house that sat alone in the night.

"Well, if it isn't Burger Boy," Sandy said when Brett walked into the pizza place three nights later. "We thought you'd died."

"Hey," Dooley called. "Where have you been? I thought we'd be seeing more of you, not less. Was it something I said?"

Brett shrugged off their good-natured teasing. He was lonely. He missed Shayla, but she hadn't called since the night of the boat ride, and he wasn't sure she ever would again. "I've been working," he said, picking up a pool cue. "Who wants to lose to me first?"

"Me," Sandy said. BJ gave her a puppy-dog look that told Brett BJ liked her as more than a friend.

Dooley said, "Actually, I'm glad you stopped by because the bunch of us are planning to drive out to Cape Cod for a clambake on the beach next Sunday. Interested in coming?"

"What's a clambake?"

"We bury clams and lobsters in the sand on

top of hot rocks and seaweed, and hours later we have some majorly good eating."

"I don't know," Brett said, then just as quickly changed his mind. Why not? It wasn't as if he had anything else to do. "Count me in," he amended.

Minutes later, he was leaning over the table, aligning his cue stick, when Dooley asked, "Who's the babe in the doorway staring at you?"

Brett glanced up and saw Shayla. She looked scared. He dropped the stick, bounded across the room, and caught her in his arms. "You're here! I don't believe it."

"I—I missed you. And I've thought a lot about the things you said."

By now the others had crowded around them.

"Are you Shayla Brighton?" Susan asked. "Oh my gosh! We were in fourth grade together. I wanted you to come outside at recess and play with me, but you never could. I used to go home and cry because I felt so sad about you not being able to ever come out in the sunshine." Susan's eyes filled with tears, as if to underscore her confession.

Shayla touched Susan's shoulder. "I remember you. You were nice to me, and I used to watch you and the other girls play through the window. Thank you." Then she gave BJ a contemptuous glare. "I'm Ghost Girl."

BJ's face turned beet red, and he said, "Sorry about that."

"This is my girl," Brett told the others, feeling a surge of pride.

"You dog," Dooley said to Brett. "No wonder you've been busy nights." Dooley grinned at Shayla. "You shoot pool?"

"No," she said without taking her gaze off Brett. "But I know how to watch."

Brett looped his arm tightly around Shayla's waist. He wasn't going to let go of her again.

Brett was soaring on an adrenaline rush when he coasted into the driveway at three in the morning. Things couldn't have gone better for him and Shayla that night. The kids she'd shunned for so long had been fascinated with her. And captivated too. After shooting a few games of pool, they'd headed back to Dooley's house, where they'd watched a video and eaten large bowls of popcorn. When Brett had finally taken Shayla home, she told him, "I'm glad I came tonight."

"Just the first of many," he said.

She gave him a longing look he puzzled over, but she scooted out of the car and darted inside her house before he could ask her about it. Now, back at the cabin, he only recalled what it had felt like to be a couple, to have Shayla to wrap his arms around and snuggle against.

Brett slid open the patio door he always used when entering late at night, locked it behind him, and crept toward his bedroom. Suddenly the room blazed with light. His mother sat in a chair, facing the door, her eyes shooting fire. In a low, growling voice, she asked, "What's going on, Brett? Is this how you repay my trust in you?"

Nine

Brett froze, then turned slowly to face his mother. *Busted.* "Mom, it's not what you think."

"Really?" She stood and advanced toward him. "What I think is that you're a liar and a sneak. Persuade me that you're not."

"I—um—I've been seeing someone . . . a girl."

"Well, doesn't *that* comfort me," she said sarcastically. "And what's wrong that you haven't let me meet her? How could you do this, Brett? Why?"

He knew he'd made a tactical error. He

should have told his mother about Shayla by now, but he'd been so caught up in winning Shayla, he had forgotten about most everything else. "She's not like other girls."

His mother blanched. "You're not—she's not—"

Brett grasped his mother's meaning and felt embarrassed. "We're not doing anything wrong, Mom, if that's what you're asking. And I'm sorry if I've worried you." He fidgeted under his mother's withering glare. "Um—can we sit down?"

They retreated to the sofa, where Brett struggled to gather his thoughts. "Remember when I asked Dr. Packtor about XP—where people can't go out into the sun without getting burned?"

"Yes, and you told me that there was a girl—" His mother stopped abruptly. "Is *that* the girl you're seeing? Why didn't you tell me?"

"It's taken me some time to get her to date me," he confessed. "I sort of had to wear her down."

His mother shook her head and rubbed her temples wearily. "You could have said something to me before now, son. You didn't have to sneak around. I would have understood."

"Maybe so, but it just seemed easier to keep it to myself. I didn't want anyone to know, just in case . . . you know . . . she rejected me. She was scared, Mom. Kids made fun of her when she was smaller. I—I know what it feels like to have people talking about you behind your back." He squirmed. "You're probably thinking I just feel sorry for her, but that's not true. I like her, Mom. I really like her."

She studied him, her expression softening. He'd never mentioned liking a girl to his mother before now, or the sting of rejection he'd felt during the time he adjusted to chemo while still trying to fit in at school. He was afraid she'd start on some lecture, but she surprised him and said, "I want to meet her. I'll fix dinner for the three of us."

"I'll ask her," Brett said. "Shayla's special, Mom. She doesn't deserve to have XP."

"Just like you didn't deserve to have leukemia," his mother said. "Believe me, I know, Brett—life isn't fair."

———

The night Shayla came to dinner, Brett worked feverishly to make the cabin safe for her. Because the summer sun didn't set until after nine o'clock, he didn't want her to risk exposure to damaging light. He hung sheets across windows, turned off lamps, and lit candles. His mother set the table with her finest dishes and placed candles in silver holders. Shayla drove her own car over because the windows were specially tinted. By the time she arrived, the savory smells of roast beef and potatoes filled a cabin turned into a safe haven for its guest.

"Brett tells me you're taking courses at Boston College," his mother said as the three of them ate together. "Do you have a major in mind?"

"Night work," Shayla said, then smiled, which invited Brett and his mother to smile too. "Maybe computer programming," she added. "I can work from my home that way."

Listening to them gave Brett a massive case of nerves, but as the evening progressed, he saw that Shayla and his mother were getting on well, and he relaxed. His mother even surprised him when she told them she'd clean up and they could leave. Outside, Shayla said, "Your mother's nice."

"I guess so."

"I told my parents about you and they want to meet you."

Brett got nervous all over again. He'd liked it better when it had been just him and Shayla. "All right," he said. "How about when I pick you up for the clambake?"

On the day of the clambake, it was decided that Dooley and his friends would go early to swim and play on the beach, and that Brett and Shayla would show up after the sun went down. Brett arrived at Shayla's house to face her mother and father. Her father was a baseball fan, so Brett discovered they had plenty to talk about, but despite the ease of the visit, Brett saw their apprehension when it came time to leave. He wanted to assure them he'd take good care of Shayla but didn't know how.

"First-date jitters," Shayla sighed when she and Brett were driving away. "I don't think they ever expected me to have a boyfriend from the daylight world."

"They'll just have to get used to me hanging around, because I plan to make a habit of it."

He reached over, took her hand, and held it for the long drive to the Cape.

Just as twilight descended, Brett and Shayla found their friends sitting around a small campfire on the beach. "Just in time," Dooley said, using tongs to dig through piles of seaweed for clams, lobsters, and corn on the cob from the heated pit. "Let the feast begin!"

Brett watched Shayla, shy at first, slowly warm to the others and them to her. Brett wanted to protect her, put his arms around her, ward off any hurt that might come her way, and he would have challenged anyone who treated her badly.

The night turned chilly. Dooley rebuilt the fire. Soon couples began to pair off and wander farther down the beach. Those who didn't sat around telling ghost stories.

"Come on," Brett said, taking Shayla's hand and leading her to a spot away from the others. He spread their blanket and stretched out beside her. Together they studied the stars. She pointed out the constellations, named them, and made him wonder why he'd never spent the time to learn about the night sky. He vowed he would learn all he could because night was her home in the universe, and he wanted to be where she was, live wherever she did.

"Are you having a good time?" He rose up on his elbows and gazed down at her moonlit face.

"I'm having a very good time. I never expected to be here, with them, doing this."

"You mean having a clambake?"

"No . . . belonging," she said.

His heart banged hard in his chest. The scent of her hair made him light-headed. "It's just the first of a hundred things I want to do with you."

"Beginning with—?" Her eyes seemed clear as glass, and he imagined that he could see into her very soul.

"Beginning with this." He leaned down, touched his lips to hers. She welcomed his kiss and allowed it to deepen. Suddenly it was as if a thousand fireworks had gone off in his head. Colors exploded and ricocheted in his mind; his body felt as if it were on fire. She was moonlight and starlight to him, a night vision he wanted to hold on to forever.

"I love you," he whispered into her ear.

Shayla's arms slid around his neck. "And I love you," she whispered back.

Two days later, Brett was still flying from his night on the beach with Shayla. So this was what love felt like—a rocket ride, with his heart so full of joy that he thought it would spill out of him or seep through his pores. He was humming as he prepared to go to work, when the phone rang. He picked it up and heard a woman's teary voice ask, "Is this Brett?"

"It is."

A pause. "This is Cynthia Brighton, Shayla's mother. I got your number from the information operator, thank God."

Brett felt his stomach tighten. Why would Shayla's mother be calling him? *Unless—?* "What's wrong? Is it Shayla?"

"She's in the hospital," came the answer. "It seems she went out in her boat late last night. She must have experienced engine trouble because she was stranded out in the sea for hours."

Brett felt sick. "And what happened?"

Maybe her boat had overturned. Maybe she had gotten caught in a storm.

"She was all right . . . for a while. And then . . ."

He could hear that Mrs. Brighton was having trouble controlling her voice. "And then *what*?"

"And then the sun came up."

Ten

❧

Shayla had been found unconscious, drifting out to sea in the open boat, in the hot summer afternoon. Three fishermen from a passing cabin cruiser had captured the dinghy, taken Shayla onboard, and radioed for an ambulance. Back onshore, an emergency medical team had pumped her dehydrated body full of fluids and rushed her to the area's community hospital, where she was flown to Boston Children's by a Life Force helicopter. She lay in the intensive care area of the burn unit with third-degree burns over eighty percent of her body.

Brett drove like a madman through rush-hour traffic to get there. Her parents were pacing the waiting room, distraught but subdued. Shayla's mother surprised Brett by hugging him, holding on as if for dear life. "She's asked to see you," Cynthia Brighton said.

"Is she—? Will she—?" He couldn't say the words.

"Her doctors hold no hope," Shayla's father said. "She had no defense against the sun."

Refusing to believe what he'd been told, Brett followed her parents to the bed that held Shayla. He didn't recognize her. She was swathed in wet compresses and lying on an air mattress that lifted her burned body off the surface of the bed. Thick pads covered her eyes. She was blind.

He bent down and smelled the sharp aroma of medication. "Hi, baby," he whispered into her ear.

"Brett?"

"I'm here." He wanted to touch her but knew he couldn't.

"They've given me morphine," she said. "I feel like I'm floating. It doesn't hurt now."

Emotion clogged his throat. He'd had morphine a few times during his cancer treatments, so he knew the sensation of painless weightlessness. "Why'd you go out there without me? You know I would have gone with you."

"I got an e-mail. Kimberly died. I only went out because I hurt so bad." Her voice dropped to a whisper as the pain of her loss overcame her. He knew that morphine couldn't touch that kind of pain.

"You went to the place with the rocks, didn't you?"

"I cried myself to sleep. When I woke, the tide had gone out. I was scared, Brett."

He couldn't speak, imagining her agony as the sun crawled over the horizon and began to sear her skin. She'd been helpless.

"Will you stay with me?"

"I'll stay," he managed to say.

"You rest now, honey," her mother said over Brett's shoulder. "We'll all stay."

Brett's mother rented a car to drive into Boston. As soon as she appeared in the family waiting room at the hospital, he remembered that he'd left her stranded. "Mom, I'm sorry" was all he said.

Her eyes were red-rimmed from exhaustion, but she didn't upbraid him. "I rented the car for a week," she said. "After that—"

"After that I may still be here," Brett said.

"You should think about coming home, at least to shower and change."

"There's a sleeping room and a shower here for patients' families. Shayla's parents said I could use it whenever I wanted."

His mother tried again. "The pressure of waiting can be crushing, Brett. You should take breaks."

He saw the pain in her eyes and knew she was telling him how it had been for her all the times she'd waited through his long hospital-izations and treatments. She had waited alone, miles from home, with no one by her side. At least the Brightons had each other. Brett put his arms around her. "Real men don't leave, Mom. No matter how bad it is, real men stay."

She started to cry but eventually pulled away and picked up her purse. "I'll be home if you need me," she said. She slipped a fifty-dollar bill into his hand. "For whatever you need."

He watched her walk away, seeing her life's

pattern for the first time. He was now the watcher, not the victim. Regardless, he wanted neither role.

Dooley came, and so did the others. They saw Shayla, one by one, to say goodbye.

"I had no idea they cared about me," she told Brett.

"I told you they did."

"They never would have if it hadn't have been for you."

"I love you, Shayla."

The night she died, he was beside her bed. Across the room, moonlight trickled through slats in the blinds. He watched the light shift, saw a shadow pass, heard her take a breath, stop, take another breath, then no more. He tangled his fingers in her hair, kissed her forehead, and walked out of the room, leaving her parents to mourn without him.

The drive home was quick because there was no traffic. He followed the coastal highway under the light of a full August moon. He slowed as he passed her house, stopping just long enough to stare out the car window at the brightly lit widow's walk far above the bluff.

Then he saw something move. In the pale bisque-colored light, there were two figures, a woman in a long dress and a girl with long hair. They hovered at the rail like pale white smoke, forms without substance, gazing out at the sea. Brett rubbed his eyes, looked again. The apparitions were gone. He was alone in the moonlight.

Eleven

Brett walked up the hill of the cemetery in the heat of the sun, a book clutched under his arm. Shayla's parents had given it to him after her funeral. They had supposed it was his, probably because he'd once written his name and phone number in it. He was glad to have the book because it had belonged to Shayla, the only girl he had ever loved.

He'd been at school for weeks now, going through the motions of adjusting to a life without her. His friends had been kind to him, understanding, but Brett knew it would be a very long time before he was ready to merge into the mainstream of high school life.

At the crest of the hill, he searched the grave markers and found Shayla's in the brightest, sunniest spot on the hill. Despite his sadness, he smiled, knowing that her parents had chosen it on purpose. Now Shayla could rest in the rays of the sun for all time. No need to hide in the night ever again.

Brett sat cross-legged on the green grass. Soon autumn would be coming, then winter and snow. Being from the Florida Keys, he'd never seen snow, except in movies and on TV. He looked forward to the cold white winter because it would match the way his heart felt without her.

He opened the book to his favorite poem, began to read to Shayla, and got almost to the end before tears blurred the words and made them unreadable. He shut the book. No matter . . . he knew them by heart. He touched the hot bronze metal of Shayla's grave marker. Tracing the raised letters with his fingers, he finished the poem for her from memory. He said, " 'I love thee with the breath, smiles, tears of all my life!—and, if God choose, I shall but love thee better after death.' "

BOOK TWO

Bobby's Girl

One

"**D**id I tell you that my brother Steve's coming home from college this weekend?" Bobby Harrod asked.

Sitting across from him at the library table, Dana Tafoya, Bobby's girlfriend, felt her heartbeat accelerate. "No, you didn't. Why is he coming?"

"For medical tests." Bobby tapped his pencil on his open book.

Fear shot through Dana. "What's wrong with him?"

"Don't know. That's why he's coming home. Mom wants him to see a specialist she works with at the hospital." Bobby gave Dana a quizzical look. "You feel all right? You look pale."

Dana forced a smile. "Taco regret from lunch," she lied. She couldn't let on to Bobby how hard his news had hit her. She wasn't even supposed to know his stepbrother. But she did know him. Two years before, for one magical summer, she'd known Steve Harrod very well. "What's his problem?"

"Bad headaches. Double vision. Dizzy spells. Steve kept quiet about it for as long as he could, but his coach started noticing that Steve's passing was off. He sent him to the team doc, who sent him in for tests at the hospital, but Mom wants him checked here. She says she trusts the doctors here more than in some city three hundred miles away."

Steve Harrod was a football legend in their North Carolina town, where he'd played high school ball. He had been offered scholarships to colleges and universities all over the country, but he'd chosen Florida State in Tallahassee. Now, as a junior, he was a contender for the coveted Heisman Trophy.

Dana asked, "When's he arriving?"

"Mom and Dad are picking him up at the Charlotte airport Friday night about ten o'clock. I thought I'd go too. I know that messes up our plans for going to the game and dance. Do you mind?"

"Of course I don't mind." Their high school's football team wasn't all that great anyway.

Bobby reached over and took her hand. "You want to come along for the ride?"

Dana's mind raced for an excuse not to go. "Um—no . . . I think this should be a family time."

"I don't blame you . . . since Steve's a minor deity around our house, I doubt I'll even be noticed in the backseat."

"You've always told me that you and Steve were tight."

"Only when Dad's not around."

Bobby sounded bitter, and Dana knew why. Although Bobby was his father's natural son, it was Steve who was the golden one of the family. Steve's natural father had died in a car accident when Steve was a baby. When his mother remarried, her new husband had adopted the boy. Even after Bobby was born, Steve was Mr. Harrod's favorite. But then, Steve was an extraordinary athlete and Bobby wasn't.

People automatically took a liking to the friendly, outgoing Steve, and Bobby told Dana he couldn't compete, so Dana never mentioned that she had once tumbled for Steve herself. She had thought she wouldn't have to deal with the issue until Christmas break, but now that he was coming home, there might be no way to avoid him.

"I hope whatever's wrong with Steve isn't serious," she ventured.

"Me too," Bobby said with a sigh. "He's my favorite only brother."

She smiled and squeezed his hand. "Your mom will see that he gets the best doctors."

"Dad's pretty freaked. Says he doesn't want the papers to get hold of the story because it may hurt Steve's chances at the Heisman. You'll be careful who you tell, won't you? Actually, don't tell anybody."

She hadn't considered that the news media would be interested in the story. "But won't it be noticed when Steve doesn't play Saturday?"

"The official story from FSU is that he has the flu and the sophomore quarterback will fill in for him. Fortunately, they're playing a weak team, so they should be able to keep their undefeated streak going until Steve gets back on the field."

Bobby shut his textbook. "Let's get out of here," he said to Dana. "I can't concentrate."

All the way out of the library and into the parking lot, Dana thought about seeing Steve again. What would it be like? Would he even remember her? When she'd met Steve Harrod two years before at a resort in Hilton Head, both were working. She was baby-sitting the three-year-old daughter of a business friend of her father's, and Steve was a lifeguard and recreational aide. Dana had just finished her freshman year. At sixteen, with an interest in music, she'd been a nonperson at their high school. Steve had graduated and was ready to go off to college and football camp. Her job, which lasted six weeks, had been fun, but meeting Steve and dating him had been the highlight of her summer.

Now, walking hand in hand with Bobby, she

felt guilty because she'd never told him. But she and Bobby had only begun dating a month before, at the start of their senior year. She had known he was Steve's brother—everyone knew it—although Bobby went to lengths to distance himself at school from Steve's legacy. Dana hadn't expected the two of them to be so compatible, or to have such good times together. Bobby respected her, admired her talent, encouraged her dreams. She *liked* Bobby Harrod—a lot.

"He'll be all right," she said, breaking the silence.

"Sure. I mean, nothing bad can happen to a god, can it?" Bobby opened the car door for Dana. "The one good thing about his coming home is that he'll get to meet you."

"He'll probably be too busy with his tests and wanting to get back to school. Meeting him can wait."

Bobby shut the door and leaned through the window, his face inches from hers. "No way. I *want* him to meet you. I want him to see that for once in his life he didn't get it all."

Dana felt her face redden. "Now, Bobby . . ."

"No, it's true." He kissed her quickly. "This

time I lucked out. This time Bobby got the pretty girl."

After Bobby dropped her off at home, Dana went straight to the piano. Her parents were working late. Alone, she sat for an hour playing music that usually had the power to soothe her. She finally gave up, went to her room, and rummaged through her closet for the box that held the treasured memorabilia she'd been collecting ever since the first grade. She found the ribbon from her first piano competition, when she was six, and ticket stubs from when she'd gone to New York with her parents to hear Richard Goode, one of the world's greatest classical pianists, play at Carnegie Hall.

She dug out the manila envelope filled with keepsakes from that magic summer and examined each item tenderly—the torn ticket stubs from her movie dates with Steve, a candy wrapper he'd discarded and she'd retrieved, photos of the two of them building a sand castle on the beach and playing in the pool. Her favorite was the one of them with their arms around each other that a passerby had snapped for them. Steve's blond hair glinted in the sunlight, and Dana's expression was one of pure joy.

She thought back to the day they met. She had discovered a piano in one of the banquet rooms, so during her free time, she practiced. On that particular rainy afternoon, she looked up and saw Steve standing at the doorway, listening. She'd recognized him immediately.

"Don't stop," he said. "It's beautiful."

She felt tongue-tied.

He came over and leaned his elbows on the top of the piano. "I'll bet you've played all your life."

"Since I was four. I've always loved it." Just being in Steve's presence caused her hands to tremble on the keys.

"You've got a gift. Do you mind if I listen?"

"I'm finished for today." She explained about her sitter job and how she was expected back in her room before dinner.

"Will you play again tomorrow?"

"I have to. I want to attend Juilliard someday. Only the best get to go there, so I practice all I can." She felt as if she were babbling. Why should he care about her life story?

His grin looked like warm honey. "Bet you'll make it . . . I don't know your name."

"Dana Marie," she said, using her first and middle names only.

"I'm Steve. Until tomorrow, then."

She smiled and left the room quickly, her heart banging against her chest.

True to his promise, he came the next day, and the day after that, until they were seeing each other every day and then every free minute. By the end of her vacation job, Dana had fallen madly, hopelessly in love with Steve Harrod, Bobby's only brother.

Two

Dana never told anyone, not even her best friend, Terry Brown, about her summer with Steve. Terry would have spread it all over school at the beginning of sophomore year, and Dana would have been the topic of gossip. Plus, a lot of people would never believe her in the first place, and she didn't want to be in the position of having to defend her story. Nor was it likely that she and Steve would ever cross paths again. It had simply been easier to keep it to herself, to store the memories inside her special box. And inside her heart.

The phone rang and she answered it.

"I miss you," Bobby said.

She laughed. "You just dropped me off."

"Not true. That was hours ago. What're you doing?"

Feeling guilty, she tucked the photo of herself and Steve back into the envelope. "I just finished piano practice. How about you?"

"Trying to keep my cool—I just had a big run-in with Dad. My parents lied to me, Dana."

"About what?" She immediately thought of Steve.

"They've always told me I could go to college anywhere I wanted, but now they're saying they can't afford to send me to Cal Tech. They're saying if I want to go to college all the way out in California, I'll have to get a scholarship. I've already been accepted at Cal Tech, pending my SAT scores," he added hotly, "and now they're saying they can't pay for it."

"Oh, Bobby, I'm really sorry."

"If only I played football, I'd have it made."

"Math majors are offered scholarships too."

"Jocks get more offers. Steve was drowning in scholarship offers, and Dad was hanging on to every recruiter who came in the door. He managed Steve's offers like the world's most important business deal. But as for me—well, he forgets to mention that there's no money to send *me* to college. I'm a loser, Dana. In every way, a loser."

"You've got to start believing in yourself, Bobby. Your dreams are no less valuable than your brother's."

"That's what I said, but Dad just called me ungrateful, said that until they knew what was happening with Steve, they couldn't commit the money to send me across the country just to go to college. He said if I stay in-state, it'll be manageable." Bobby sounded despondent. "Let's face it, I'll never get to Cal Tech. I just wish Mom and Dad hadn't lied to me, Dana. They could have told me this a long time ago, before I got my hopes up."

"It's not the end of the world, Bobby. You'll figure something out because you're smart. And because you're just as good as Steve."

"Listen, I'm not dissing Steve." He sounded ashamed. "Especially now. He can't help being perfect."

"But you can help yourself by stopping the competition. Steve's life isn't so perfect right now, you know."

Bobby was silent. Finally he said, "That's why you're in my life, Dana. You keep me honest. You're right. Steve's got problems, and I just have gripes."

"You can gripe to me anytime," she told him.

But once she'd hung up, guilt grabbed her again. She'd been anything but honest with him. If she were honest, she'd have told him about her and Steve. Sooner or later, she might have to, because once they met again face to face, Steve might blurt out their shared history. Then again, he might not even remember it. Frankly, Dana couldn't decide which would hurt worse.

"Being Bobby's girl does have a few perks," Terry told Dana the next day at lunch. "I mean, getting to brush up to his brother can't be too awful."

"Did you ignore the part about the medical tests? This isn't just a quick trip home for fun, you know."

"I know, I know." Terry waved Dana off. "I was only looking at the bright side." She took a sip of her soda. "I guess Brittany will ooze out of the woodwork once she hears he's home."

Brittany Watson had been Steve's girlfriend throughout high school but had taken a job in the area after graduation instead of going to college. "Bobby told me they broke up before Steve left for FSU."

Terry rolled her eyes. "Like that ever stopped Brittany."

Steve had never lacked female attention, and for all Dana knew, his life at college was filled with pretty girls. Still, for part of one summer, she had been special to him, and that was what she wanted to remember. "Bobby doesn't talk about Steve's love life," she told Terry.

"Speaking of Bobby, here he comes," Terry said, picking up her tray. "Grab you later." She ducked away.

"I thought you were in class," Dana said when Bobby crouched beside her chair.

"Hall pass. I saw you when I passed by, and since we're heading to the airport when school's out, I won't get to talk to you until later tonight. Why don't you come over to-morrow morning? I thought we could take a swim in the pool, get some lunch."

Dana's stomach tightened. What if Steve was hanging around? "I have a piano lesson."

"No problem. I'll pick you up at Mrs. Sherrill's." Bobby stood. "Got to run."

Dana watched Bobby hurry off, knowing that she had no good excuse not to go to his house on Saturday. She'd done it often since they'd been dating. She took a deep breath. There was no way she could put off the inevitable.

Steve was with his parents at the hospital when Bobby brought Dana to the house on Saturday. She breathed a sigh of relief. With a little luck, she might miss meeting up with him altogether. She quickly changed into her bathing suit and swam several laps with Bobby before they stretched out in patio chairs to soak up the sun. Even though it was October, the cool nights gave way to warm temperatures by midday.

Dana rose on her elbow and asked, "You—um, haven't said much about picking up your brother at the airport. Did it go all right?"

"Same old, same old. Mom and Dad were all over Steve and I was invisible."

"That bad, huh?"

Bobby rolled over to look at her. "That was cold," he confessed. "Truth is, Steve looks like he's lost weight, and he's definitely not his normal self. We didn't get to talk last night because his head hurt pretty bad. He just crawled into bed as soon as he could."

The noise of the patio door sliding open startled them both. "We're back, bro," said a male voice.

Dana tensed, kept her back turned.

Bobby got up. "Good. How'd it go?"

"It went. They took X rays, but the neurologist won't see the films until Monday. I'm supposed to check in Sunday night for more tests."

"Well, come over here. There's someone I'd like you to meet."

Dana's heart hammered. Her moment of truth had arrived. She sat up, squinting because the sun was over Steve's shoulder and it glared in her eyes.

"The girl of my dreams," Bobby said, putting his hand on Dana's shoulder. "Dana, this is Steve, superstar of the Harrod family."

If Steve recognized her, it didn't show on

his face. "So you're the girl Bobby's been telling me about. Glad to finally meet you."

"I'm glad to meet you too," she said. Her voice sounded breathy. She hoped neither of them noticed.

"I didn't lie, did I?" Bobby said. "She's something else, huh?"

She felt her face redden. "Stop it, Bobby."

"She's something else all right," Steve echoed.

"Look, we're going out for a burger. Want to come along, talk to me and Dana about college and all?"

She held her breath, afraid Steve would agree to come. If he did, there would be no way she could gag down food.

"Not this time," Steve said.

"I'll go change." Dana darted to the house and hurried to the guest room, where she'd left her clothing. Her heart in her throat, she struggled into her clothes. Steve hadn't appeared to remember her. Their time together had been forgotten, probably lost among all the other girls who had come along over the years. She had worried about nothing.

Her hand shook as she brushed her long dark hair. "It's just as well," she said to herself. "It doesn't matter. It's better this way."

Suddenly she was desperate to get out of the house and away from the memories seeing Steve had stirred up. She grabbed her purse, opened the door, and stopped short.

Steve was lounging against the wall in the hallway. Their gazes met. She froze. He straightened and stepped toward her. "I think we should talk, don't you, Dana Marie?"

Three

~

"Maybe so," she said, her voice barely a whisper.

"Did you know that when I got home that summer, I called all the people with the last name of Marie in the local phone book? There are four, just in case you're wondering, but none of them had ever heard of a Dana."

She felt hot and cold all over. "I—it's my middle name."

"No lie?"

His words stung. "No lie."

"All I knew was that you were from this area, so I wondered why you made it hard for me to find you again. I went over things in my mind a hundred times, trying to figure out what I'd said or done that caused you to lie to me."

"I never lied to you."

Steve shoved his hands into the pockets of his jeans. "But you didn't tell me the whole truth either. How was I supposed to locate you when I never even knew your last name?"

Her rationale was beyond anything she could explain to herself, much less to *him*. "I— I don't know why. I was just sixteen. You were the hero of half the state, and I was a nobody. I never thought I'd ever see you again." She felt hot wetness behind her eyes. *Don't cry,* she told herself silently.

"Were you dating Bobby at the same time and just wanted to mess around behind his back? Were you afraid I might drop your name to him and spoil your cheating game?"

"No! I didn't even know Bobby then. I would never cheat on him."

"But you'll cheat on me." Steve crossed his arms. His blue eyes looked cold. "You *are* dating my brother. Didn't you think we'd eventually run into each other somewhere along the way?"

"I—I wasn't sure you'd even remember me."

"You're not so forgettable, Dana."

Tears welled in her eyes. "I—I didn't believe you could care about me. You could have any girl—"

"I didn't want just *any* girl."

She had dreamed of him saying such things to her. "If I had known—"

"Hey, what's going on here?" Bobby came down the hall, flipping his car keys. "You trying to snake my girl, bro?"

Steve turned. "Just getting acquainted," he said easily. "Dana tells me she plays the piano."

"Like a pro," Bobby said.

Dana looked away, feeling like a kid caught stealing.

"You sure you don't want to grab a burger with us?"

"Not this time," Steve said.

Bobby put his arm around Dana. "Listen, I know you'll head back to FSU as soon as you can, but when you're home this summer, maybe we can do stuff together. That is, if you can find a girl." He grinned impishly.

Steve punched Bobby playfully on the shoulder. "I'll see what I can do." He backed up. "Nice meeting you, Dana. You take good care of my brother, you hear? If you don't, I'll come looking for you."

Dana smiled weakly. She let Bobby take her hand and walk her down the hall. Her knees felt rubbery all the way to the car parked in the driveway.

Once she got home, Dana played the piano for almost two hours.

"Don't wear out the keys," her mother said, passing through the living room.

"I want to be sharp for state competition," Dana said.

"But that's not until spring."

"And it's my best chance to get noticed by the Juilliard people."

"It's still a long way off."

Dana turned on the piano bench. "Most mothers are begging their kids to practice. I didn't mean to annoy you."

"Whoa. I never said you were annoying me. I was just wondering why you were driving yourself today. Did you and Bobby have a fight?"

Her mother knew Dana's habit of playing when she was upset or needed space to work out a problem, so Dana wasn't surprised by the question, only annoyed. "Bobby and I are fine. His brother's home from college having some medical tests run, and his family's concerned."

"What's wrong with him?"

"He's been having really bad headaches."

"That's too bad, but I don't see how it concerns you."

Dana hit discordant keys on the piano, pushed back the bench, and stood. "I'm Bobby's girlfriend, Mom, and he's worried about his older brother. Why wouldn't it affect me? I think the world of Bobby."

Her mother looked startled. "Sorry, I didn't mean to upset you. Just keep playing. Pretend I never interrupted."

Dana shook her head. "I'm finished." She headed up the stairs to her bedroom. She felt anxious and tense. Since her conversation with Steve, her mind had been in turmoil, her insides in a knot. She still adored him; the old feelings hadn't changed. Except that now she was Bobby's girl, and no amount of piano playing was going to chase away her predicament.

Bobby asked Dana to a family cookout on Sunday. "Steve's checking into the hospital at six, so this is the big feast before he begins a diet of hospital food."

"I—um, have to study."

"The cookout won't last long."

"I can't."

Bobby lifted her chin and stared into her eyes. "Hey, what's wrong? You haven't been yourself the past couple of days."

"Nothing's wrong. I've just got a big test this week I need to study for."

Bobby looked hurt. "You're not getting tired of us, are you?"

"Why would you ask me that? Why are you so insecure? I have a test. Can't I be thinking about something else besides *us* all the time?"

"Low blow," he said, throwing up his hands like a shield. "I guess because I think about you all the time, I want you to think about me all the time too. But you've got a point. It's not fair and I'm a jerk and I'm sorry. Forgive me?"

He looked so appealingly pathetic that she

had to smile. "I didn't mean to sound angry," Dana said. "Terry would kill to have her boyfriend think of her instead of soccer season, so I'm not complaining."

"And I didn't mean to come across like some kind of desperate dope. This thing with Steve's got me down. His headaches are scary, Dana. I heard him moaning through my bedroom wall last night because his head hurt so much."

She shuddered. What she really wanted was to be with Steve. But she'd forfeited that privilege. "Why don't you come over after Steve checks in? We'll sit on the porch swing and talk."

"Will you hold my hand?" Bobby looked winsomely optimistic.

"Maybe." Her irritation melted. She just couldn't stay mad at him.

"Will you let me kiss you?"

"Don't push your luck."

He dipped his head, kissed her quickly on the mouth, then bounded off the porch. "Too late," he called. "The kissing *bandito* strikes again." He got into his car. "See you tomorrow."

She watched him drive off, her thoughts returning to Steve. She wasn't sure how she was going to get through the next few days, but she would. And she would do everything in her power not to hurt Bobby, unwittingly caught between two people who loved him and who, because of him, could never be together again.

Four

"I should be at the hospital with Mom and Dad." Bobby caught Dana in the hall between classes Monday morning.

"Why aren't you?"

"Dad made me come to school. Said I'd just be in the way. Like I can concentrate on classes when my brother's going through all that."

Hank Harrod's insensitivity toward Bobby irked Dana, but she didn't want to worsen Bobby's already glum mood, so she kept her thoughts about him to herself. "How long will Steve be in the hospital? You can visit him after school, you know."

"I know, but I'd wanted to spend the day with him. What's so hard about my dad understanding that?" Just as the tardy bell sounded, he said, "Come with me today."

"To the hospital?" Dana froze.

He gave her a puzzled look. "Well, yeah, to the hospital."

"I don't think—"

"I'll pick you up at the south entrance at three. I'm out of here!"

With a sinking feeling, Dana watched him sprint down the hall. He hadn't even heard her begging off. She realized that she'd have to go with him, and she both wanted it and dreaded it. She reminded herself that in a few days, Steve would be back at FSU, and she wouldn't have to think about seeing him again until the holidays. Maybe by then she could get him out of her system once and for all.

"Hey, bro." Bobby sauntered into Steve's room that afternoon, Dana by his side.

Steve's face lit up. "Hey yourself." He was sitting up on the side of his bed, flipping through TV channels with the remote. He wore jeans, the usual hospital gown that tied behind his neck, and a blue plastic bracelet that identified him as a patient. He looked tanned, fit, and healthy. "Pull up some chairs."

"Where're the folks?"

"Cruising the cafeteria."

"You remember Dana, don't you?"

Steve swept her with his clear blue eyes. "How could I forget her?"

Bobby slid two chairs alongside the bed and sat in one. Dana nervously took the other. "Do you know anything yet?" Bobby asked.

"The neurosurgeon Mom wants on my case had an emergency today, but he's supposed to stop by in the morning with some sort of information about my tests. After that, I'm coming home."

"Sorry I couldn't hang here today. Dad made me go to school."

"It would have been totally boring," Steve said. "Nothing but blood work and an MRI and a whole lot of waiting in between. I'll bet they took a hundred shots of my brain."

"You have one?" Bobby deadpanned.

"Not the size of yours." Steve grinned, then turned his attention to Dana. "What did Bobby promise to make you come see me? Dinner at McDonald's?"

She cleared her throat. "I wanted to come. I wanted to see how you're doing . . . wish you luck."

"Very nice of you."

She heard a hint of sarcasm in his voice.

"You ever get those SAT scores back?" Steve returned his attention to his brother. "I know you have a lot riding on them."

"Not yet. Probably in a few months."

"You'll do well on the test. Better than I did, for sure."

"Not that it'll be noticed like if I played football."

Steve groaned. "Give it up. Brains always wins over brawn. Don't you think so, Dana?"

She started, not having expected Steve to talk to her, much less put her on the spot. "Talent is talent," she said after a pause. "The area doesn't matter, only drive and determination."

Bobby winked at her.

Steve said, "You know, there's a piano in the rec room downstairs. I'd like to hear you play, Dana."

She felt her face redden. Why didn't Steve back off and stop baiting her? She stood. "Sure. I can do that."

Bobby sprang up beside her. "You're really going to be impressed, Stevie."

"I'll leave a note for Mom and Dad." Steve scribbled a message on a piece of paper and propped it on his pillow.

The three of them went down the hall, took the elevator, and found their way to a spacious recreation room. Dana was seething, but she stared straight ahead, refusing to meet Steve's eyes even while Bobby told him about her goal of attending the Juilliard School after she graduated. *He already knows,* she thought, wishing Bobby would drop her as a topic of conversation.

In the rec room, several patients were reading. Two others were playing a game of cards.

"Would any of you object to some piano music?" Steve asked boldly.

They all nodded consent and Dana sat at the piano, determined to focus on the music and not her anger. She ran the scales and was surprised to hear that the instrument was tuned. "Any requests?" she asked, looking Steve in the face for the first time that evening.

"How about the *Moonlight* Sonata?"

She stiffened. That was the piece she was

playing when he'd first met her at Hilton Head. "Beethoven called it *Sonata quasi una fantasia*," Dana said. "He wrote it in 1801 when he first learned he might be going deaf. Is that the piece you mean?"

"She knows everything," Bobby whispered to Steve, obviously pleased by Dana's quick response and thorough knowledge of classical music.

"That's the piece," Steve said.

"You shock me, Steve. I thought you only listened to heavy metal and rock," Bobby kidded.

"I developed a taste for classical a few summers ago. I just never told you."

Dana struck the keys, pulling the melody out of her mind and fingers and pouring it into the old piano. Instantly the music filled the room, swept the air with its haunting notes. Soon she forgot everything except the magic of Beethoven's wonderful melody. She played it start to finish, and when the final notes faded into silence, she heard the sound of applause behind her. She turned and was shocked to see that a small crowd had gathered.

"Heavenly," a nurse said. "I was just walking down the hall, and I had to come inside and see who could make this old thing produce such music."

An elderly man wiped his cheeks.

"What a gift you have," said another man.

"Thank you," Steve said softly, simply. "It was beautiful."

Dana felt self-conscious.

"Her name's Dana Tafoya," Bobby announced to the listeners. "And someday she'll play at Carnegie Hall. Just wait and see."

"I'll buy a ticket," Steve said.

Dana lost sight of him as people gathered around her, enthusiastically congratulating her on the impromptu performance. A man in a business suit thrust a business card into her hand. "I'm the volunteer coordinator here. Have you ever considered being a volunteer? If you'd come in even once a month and play for our shut-ins, it would make a world of difference for them."

"I—I—"

"Will you please consider it? Call me anytime and I'll set it up. I know it's not Carnegie

Hall," he said with a laugh, "but you could do our patients a whole lot of good with your musical talent."

Bobby slipped his arm around Dana's waist. "I'm her manager." He grinned. "And we'll get back to you."

The group laughed. Dana smiled too. It felt good to have her work enjoyed. Isn't that what she'd always wanted? To play concerts and have people appreciate beautiful classical music? "I'll see what I can work out," she said.

When the people had drifted away, Bobby hugged her. Over his shoulder, she saw Steve staring at them. She closed her eyes, wishing that the brothers could trade places, knowing it would never happen. She was Bobby's girl now.

Five

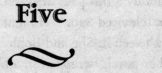

Steve and Bobby's parents came into the room minutes later. "We got your note," Hank Harrod said.

"And we heard all about your piano playing from the people who were leaving," Martha Harrod said to Dana. "Sorry we missed it."

"Rain check," Bobby said.

Mr. Harrod turned to Steve. "You must be feeling better."

"I feel fine when I don't have a headache. And being stuck in that room upstairs isn't much fun."

"You'll see Dr. Patelli in the morning," his

mother said. "I'm sure he'll have some answers for us."

"Hope so. I need to get back to the field. We barely won this past weekend." The game had been televised Saturday night on ESPN. Dana hadn't seen it. She and Bobby had sat together on her porch, wrapped in a blanket, watching the stars come out.

His father hooked an arm around Steve's shoulders. "That freshman who replaced you stunk. Couldn't hit the side of a barn with his passes. The defense saved his cookies."

They started walking and discussing the game. Martha had gone around them, reaching the elevator ahead of them and pushing the button. Bobby stood in the hall with Dana, as if forgotten by his family.

Dana watched his lively and animated expression sag. Pity and disgust toward his parents mingled in her. How could they be so blind to his feelings? She slipped her hand into his. "Want to buy a girl a Coke? She's pretty thirsty after all that piano playing."

He blinked, as if remembering suddenly where he was and who was with him. "I was flashing back to middle school," he said apologetically. "Steve had just thrown the touchdown pass that won the league championship. Mom and Dad were so excited that they forgot me at the field. I was hanging with some other guys in the upper part of the stadium, and the next thing I knew, the car had left the parking lot following after the rest of the team, honking and cheering. They were all the way to the pizza place before Steve asked, 'Where's Bobby?'" Bobby sighed. "Dad came back for me, and he was really mad because it was my responsibility to keep up. I guess I've just never been good at keeping up."

Dana touched her forehead to Bobby's chest. "Then you can keep up with me. And right now I have to go home. But I demand a soda first."

He offered her a sad smile. "What would I do without you, Dana? You're everything to me."

Dana's phone rang after eleven that night. She grabbed it, knowing her mother didn't like her getting calls that late. Bobby knew it too, so she was prepared to remind him when a voice said, "Hi, Dana."

Her breath caught. It wasn't Bobby. "Hi, Steve."

"I know it's late," Steve said. "I hope you weren't asleep."

"No, just studying."

"I felt I should call and say I'm sorry."

"For what?"

"For giving you a hard time every time I see you. I haven't been very nice to you, and that's not right."

Her hand squeezed the receiver. "No, you haven't," she said. "You made me pretty mad at you tonight."

"I figured I did. No excuses except it was a real shock to walk out on the patio that day and discover that the one girl I'd always wanted to meet up with again was dating my brother."

"I like Bobby. He's been good to me."

"And he's crazy about you, so don't worry, I'm not going to rock the boat."

Relief mingled with regret. "I wouldn't hurt him for the world."

"Neither would I."

"He worships you, you know. And he feels neglected, left out." She believed Steve was in a position to help Bobby with his relationship with their parents, especially with their dad.

"I know. I've tried for years to get Dad to pay more attention to Bobby, but I guess it's still not happening."

"No, it isn't."

Steve sighed heavily. "What's ironic is that Bobby has nothing to feel inferior about. He's really smart."

"But he's not an athlete."

"I still don't know why that matters so much to him. When we were kids, he used to do my math assignments. I remember a time when I was eight and Bobby was only four. He poured out Mom's face powder and wrote some addition problems in the dust. I got a licking because nobody believed that a four-year-old could have done the math." Steve chuckled. "He felt really bad about me getting into trouble and told Mom he learned how to add and subtract watching *Sesame Street*. The truth is he's always been a whiz. All I can do is play football. I'd have traded some of my athletic skills for some of his smarts many times."

Dana felt herself softening. It would have been better if she could have stayed angry at Steve, but she couldn't, and she felt torn between her loyalty to Bobby and her feelings for Steve. "I know Bobby's smart. Too bad your dad can't appreciate him."

"He's lucky to have you. Very lucky."

Her mouth felt as dry as cotton. "I'm really sorry about your headaches. I hope you'll be all right."

"I will. Thanks for playing tonight. I'd forgotten how good you were."

She was flattered. "I was mad at you when I started playing, but I got over it once I got into the music."

He laughed. "That coordinator was all over you about playing for the shut-ins. It was nice of you to say you'd try to work it out."

"How can I pass up the opportunity to be in front of a real live audience?"

"I'll miss you when I go back to school."

"Same here," she said before thinking. She bit her lower lip as silence lengthened between them.

Finally Steve said, "But you're Bobby's girl now."

"Yes," she answered, swallowing around a lump in her throat. "I'm Bobby's girl now."

Dana was sitting in class the next morning, listening to a boring lecture, when Bobby suddenly appeared in the doorway.

"Can I help you, Mr. Harrod?" the teacher asked.

"I have to talk to Dana Tafoya. It's an emergency."

Bobby looked pale and frantic. Dana grew alarmed.

"I have a pass," Bobby said, waving a piece of paper. "Please."

The teacher nodded and Dana scooted out the door. The hall was empty. "I'm on my way to the hospital." Bobby's eyes looked wild.

"What's wrong?" Dana's heart hammered and her mouth went dry.

"It's Steve," Bobby said, a tremor in his voice. "He got his diagnosis. He's got brain cancer, Dana, and it's going to kill him."

Six

~

"Steve said there is a tumor pressing against his optic nerve. That's why he's having double vision. He told me that the cancer has spread to other parts of his brain, that there's nothing they can do for him." Bobby clenched and unclenched his fists.

Dana felt woozy, as if air had been sucked from the hallway. "There must be some mistake."

"No mistake." Bobby's fingers dug into her shoulders, but she welcomed the pain because it kept her from screaming. Bobby said, "Steve told me himself. He wants me down there, so

I'm going right now. I only stopped long enough to tell you."

"But isn't there anything the doctors can do? Anything at all?"

"That's what I'm going to go check out for myself. How can his doctors not be able to help him? He's only twenty years old. He's too young to die!" Bobby looked down the hallway anxiously. "I've got to go, all right?"

"Go," she said, and watched him jog to the stairwell and disappear downward. Shaking, she flattened her back against the wall and felt the cool, smooth surface through her clothes. She blinked back tears, her mind spinning. She gathered her strength and returned to the classroom with tears streaming down her face.

"Dana, what is it?" her teacher asked, alarmed.

She didn't answer. Aware that every eye in the room was on her, but not caring, she scooped up her books and fled.

"Is it true? Is Bobby's brother really dying?" Terry asked. She had come straight over to Dana's house the minute school was out.

Dana was sorry she'd gone to the door. She wasn't up to conversation. She had come straight home from school, darkened her room, and lain on her bed and cried. Now, hours later, she still felt like crying. "I'm waiting to hear from Bobby again," she told the inquisitive Terry.

"Oh, man—this really sucks. It's all over school too."

"Who told?"

"Are you kidding? It's major news, Dana. Everyone knows."

Dana was still unclear how that could be, but she was too devastated to dwell on it.

Terry asked, "So do you want me to hang around till you talk to Bobby?"

"I'll be okay. You don't have to stay."

Terry looked disappointed. "Um—can I say something?"

"Can I ever stop you from saying something?"

Sheepishly Terry said, "Point taken. Listen, I can understand your being upset about this, but, well . . . it isn't like this is happening to Bobby, you know. It's his brother, not Bobby, your boyfriend."

"What's your point?"

Terry shrugged and looked uncomfortable. "You're just taking it awfully hard, that's all. I mean it's a bad thing and all, but it isn't Bobby who's got cancer."

First her mother, now Terry. This was the second time her reactions concerning Steve had been noticed. Dana steadied herself. She couldn't blurt out her secret. "Maybe I am overreacting," she told Terry. "I can't help it. I know how much Bobby loves his brother, and I don't know how he's going to handle it. Or how I'm going to help him through it. I—I'm scared."

Terry nodded sympathetically. "I guess you just have to hang tough. Bobby doesn't need you falling apart, does he?"

Terry made perfect sense, but Dana wasn't positive she could stand on the sidelines playing the observer. She wanted to see Steve. She wanted to be with him again. "I'll try to keep my composure," she said to Terry. "My piano teacher's always telling me that. 'Dana, keep your composure no matter how badly a recital is going. Nobody likes a messy scene,' " Dana quoted Mrs. Sherrill. "So that's what I'll do.

I'll keep it together for Bobby's sake." *And for mine,* she added silently. It would do no one any good if she fell to pieces. Questions might be asked. And Dana knew she could give no plausible answers as to why Steve meant so much to her when everyone knew she belonged to Bobby.

The news hit the paper and the newscasts the following morning. Hank Harrod was furious and even took a swing at a reporter who tried to corner him to get his reaction on Steve's diagnosis. "How do you think I feel?" Hank yelled, and then aimed a punch at the reporter's face. His move was captured on camera and shown on the six o'clock news.

"Dad's mad at the world right now," Bobby told Dana over the phone that evening. "He's forbidden us to talk to anybody about Steve."

"Is that hard for you?"

"Not really. Believe it or not, this is as close as this family's been in years," Bobby confessed. "We've circled the wagons around Steve to protect him, and I feel like part of a team." He gave a mirthless laugh. "Doesn't seem right that my brother has to be dying before I become a member of the family, does it?"

Bobby remained out of school, and at midweek, Steve's coach flew in from Florida, which also made the news. The coach held a brief news conference at which he expressed his deepest regret and asked the media to back off and give Steve and his family some space. He also revealed that Steve had decided not to return to FSU and that he would be sorely missed by the team and the university.

Dana was frantic to see Steve, but she knew she couldn't rush over to the house as soon as he came home from the hospital. She bided her time. Her opportunity came one sunny October afternoon a week later. Steve's parents were at work, and Bobby, who had returned to school, was staying late because he was on the team chosen for the annual high school Brain Bowl battle. The contest would happen in March, and the physics teacher wanted Jackson High to make a good showing, so he held practice rounds after school twice a week.

Dana drove to the house, parked in the driveway, and rang the doorbell. No one answered. She screwed up her courage and went around to the backyard. Steve was sitting on the patio, staring into the cool depths of the pool. She took a deep breath to calm herself and opened the gate. As she came toward the patio, her footsteps crunched over the fallen leaves.

Steve looked up; his tortured expression softened. Shaking with emotion, she walked toward him, stopped in front of his chair, and dropped to her knees. Dana took hold of his hands and kissed them. Wordlessly, he reached out to cradle her cheek in his palm.

She closed her eyes as he laced his fingers through hers. She felt the warmth of the sun on her back, the familiar touch of his hand on her skin, and for a moment, time stood still. She longed to stop the world from spinning, longed to hold autumn captive, push away tomorrow, and live forever in this slice of time. She could not. She could not hold on to him, and she could not let go. Gently, tenderly, she laid her cheek against his lap and wept.

Seven

~

Steve pulled her up onto his lap, held her close, and rested his head against the hollow of her throat. "I knew you'd come."

"As soon as I could," she told him. "I've been going crazy."

"Don't cry." Steve brushed tears from her cheek. "Not for me."

"Then who else? Myself?" She nestled in his arms. "Talk to me. Tell me your doctors are doing something—anything to help you."

"I'm starting radiation treatments, which are supposed to shrink the tumor, but my type of tumor grows fast and is almost impossible to treat. Plus the MRI shows that the cancer's already spreading to other areas of my brain."

"How about chemotherapy?"

"It wouldn't help with my case."

His doctors had robbed him of hope, and that made her angry. "What about the headaches?"

"I have a potent painkiller for when they get really bad."

"Tell me what to expect, Steve. Please. Tell me everything."

"They expect me to go blind."

She shuddered in his arms.

"After a while, I won't be able to stand up or keep my balance. I'll start forgetting things, like how to feed myself, how to breathe. Eventually, I'll go into a coma and die. Which sounds better to me than being some kind of human vegetable."

"Oh, Steve . . . it's all so cruel." Her voice caught. She couldn't imagine his muscular body wasted away and bedridden. She couldn't accept that his smile would no longer light his face.

"I'm glad they've been honest with me. I'm glad they didn't lie and give me false hope.

That would have been worse for me. It's like a game plan in football," he said. "Once you know the plan, you can follow it. You know what to expect, what's coming next. I just have to keep my cool, follow the course."

"How long?"

He shrugged. "A few months, maybe more."

"So you're not going back to school?"

"What would be the point?" He shook his head. "No. I'll wait here. This is home. My family's here. And so are you."

"I—I'm sorry . . . so sorry . . ."

"I told them I didn't want to die in the hospital. Mom's contacted a hospice so that I can stay at home until the end." His voice was flat, matter-of-fact. "I've been to the radiologist, and he's taken me through the preliminaries. I start treatments tomorrow afternoon, five times a week for six weeks. The tumor will shrink, give me a reprieve."

"I'm glad you'll be close by. I couldn't stand it if this was happening to you and you were far away."

"My parents are taking it really hard—especially Dad. Bobby's mad too. Finally he and

Dad are in agreement about something. They're both angry because the doctors can't do much to help me. Bobby wants to help by going on the Web and tracking down some miracle cure, and Dad's all for it. There is no miracle cure, Dana. And I don't know how to tell my kid brother that the only help I want is more time with his girlfriend."

She wept for both of them, for his plans and dreams never to be fulfilled, for herself because he was being taken away so completely. Together they sat in the fading warmth of the sunlight, watching shadows lengthen across the yard. A breeze broke a few fading leaves from the treetops, and they spiraled downward, hitting the patio like teardrops.

"I want to quit school and stay at home with Steve, but Mom won't let me," Bobby told Dana a few days later, while they were on her front porch. They had carved a jack-o'-lantern together, and Bobby was wrapping the mess from the pumpkin in newspapers. "Mom and Dad are planning on doing flex time at their jobs so they can be at home more, but they won't let me do the same thing. I think it stinks."

"I'm sure Steve won't let you either." Dana set the grinning pumpkin at the top corner of the steps, loathing its artificial smile. "Quitting school and hanging around the house won't change anything."

"When things get really bad, when Steve's dying, they can't stop me."

"They probably won't stop you then." Ever since her talk with Steve, an incredible lethargy had hung over Dana like a shadow. She felt as if she'd been shut up in a dark, windowless room with stale air and no sound. Not even music could break through the heaviness inside her heart. She kept feeling Steve's arms around her but seeing Bobby's face whenever she closed her eyes.

Bobby said, "You know who called him the other night? Brittany, his old girlfriend."

Dana felt as if Bobby had twisted the pumpkin-carving knife in her. "What did she want?"

"To come see him. He said no. He says he doesn't want people coming by to stare at him like he's a freak. He doesn't look so good right now anyway. The radiologist shaved his head and marked it up with blue ink to help the doc line up the machine to zap the tumor. For all the good it'll do," he added bitterly.

"It's only hair," she said.

"He doesn't care about his hair. He just doesn't like feeling pathetic and having people talking about him. I don't blame him. All his life everybody's admired him, talked about how great he was, but now—well, things are different. I bought him a baseball cap, and he wears it whenever he goes out." Bobby sounded pleased.

"Good idea." Without meeting Bobby's gaze, she added, "Did I tell you? I'm starting to play the piano at the hospital two afternoons a week. The hospital's posting signs on every floor so that any patient who's ambulatory can sit in and listen."

"I'll go with you."

"Um—it's the same afternoons you have Brain Bowl."

"Oh." He sounded disappointed, then brightened. "That's all right, I guess. We'll both be tied up at the same time."

"Yes, that's what I was thinking too."

"You're not going to stop dating me because of Steve, are you?" Bobby asked.

She started. "Why would I do that?"

"I don't know. I'm just feeling helpless and useless watching Steve go through this and all. Maybe you don't want to be around all this sadness. I wouldn't blame you."

She went to him. "I won't leave you, Bobby."

Bobby wrapped his arms around her. He whispered, "I don't know what I'd do without you, Dana. I love you so much."

She didn't answer but held him, closing her eyes to shield him from her own pain.

Dana played her first concert to a room filled with people in wheelchairs and hospital gowns. When she was finished, and after the applause had died, she promised to return on Thursday and began gathering up her music. The room had almost cleared when she saw Steve in the back by the door. Her heart leaped.

"That was great," he said. "I could listen to you play for hours."

"Thanks. I was playing for you, don't you know?"

He touched the bill of his cap. "Sorry about the hat, but my head looks like a road map."

She smiled. "Does it matter? You're still the same on the inside."

His smile faded. "No, I'm not." He took her music. "Can you come with me?"

"Where?"

"To a place I'd like you to see. But we have to hurry because the sun's going down soon."

She followed him in her car to the outskirts of the city, into the countryside, and down a bumpy dirt road. He stopped at a clearing near a creek and got out. She let him lead her up a dirt trail to a jutting rock that hung over the water. Colorful leaves blanketed the ground and floated in the sluggish water. Snippets of a cerulean blue sky shone through the trees, and sunlight sparkled on the water like little jewels.

The beauty of the setting took her breath away, made her ache for all the autumns he would never have.

He sat beside her on the rock and took her hand. "I found this place a few years ago. I'd come and swim, spend time by myself. It's where I make all my great decisions, where I solve all my life problems. I've never shown it to another person."

She was flattered. "It's beautiful. Thank you for bringing me."

"Some life decisions need input from other people."

"Like what?"

Steve looked across the creek into a stand of trees. "I want to be with you, Dana."

Her pulse quickened. "I want to be with you, too," she confessed, "but—"

"But neither of us wants to hurt Bobby." He finished the sentence for her. "I love my brother too. And you and I both understand his demons. Once I'm gone, he'll have no one to champion him except you. So I'm not asking you to choose between us."

"What then?"

"Whenever you're able, whenever you can, come to me. I know I'm asking a lot. I know you'll be taking a risk. And I know it isn't fair to put this kind of pressure on you, but I can't help it. I don't have a whole lot of time left, and I want to spend as much of it as I can with you. Is that too much to ask?"

Steve was asking her to lead a double existence for the short duration of his life. It meant telling lies. It meant deceiving Bobby. He didn't deserve it. But Steve didn't deserve to die either. She had a decision to make, and she knew Steve would accept whatever it was.

Dana took a deep, shuddering breath and touched Steve's shoulder. He turned toward her and she moved into his arms.

"I love you," he said.

"And I love you," she whispered.

The rays of the setting sun sparked the water like fire, and as their lips met, Dana set her mind and her heart on a course from which there'd be no turning back.

Eight

❧

For the next month, Dana felt as if she were living her life in parallel universes. In one, she went to school, took piano classes, dated Bobby, remained an ordinary girl aiming toward graduation and attending college at the Juilliard School. In the other, she spent long afternoons with Steve, holding on to him, afraid to let go of him, certain that if she did, he'd be swallowed up by the black hole where his star had once shone.

They met at the hospital after Steve's treatments, after her mini-concerts for the patients. They met on Sunday afternoons when she was supposed to be in the library studying.

Sometimes she skipped school and they met where they could be alone—his favorite spot in the woods until the weather turned cold, then at her house when her parents were at work. They folded themselves into the comfort of each other's presence. Often she played the piano for him, always ending with the *Moonlight* Sonata because it was his favorite. Sometimes they sat and watched fire dance in the fireplace, sometimes they talked, often they didn't. Neither spoke of the future. He loved her and she loved him. When they were together, nothing else mattered. All they had was the here and now. It was enough because it *had* to be.

The radiation worked its wonders. Steve's tumor shrank, his headaches vanished, and his spirits rose. On Thanksgiving Day, he tossed a football with his father and Bobby in the backyard. Dana had come over to sample desserts because Bobby had begged her to. She felt awkward being around both brothers, but Steve was very careful to treat her casually, as if she were just another one of Bobby's friends.

"Maybe the doctors made a mistake," Dana

heard Hank Harrod say. "It's happened before, you know. I saw a story on TV about a woman with cancer that vanished, just like that."

"Doctors make mistakes all the time," Bobby said, going back for a pass from his father. "You might just be cured, bro." The ball spiraled downward, and Bobby kept backing up. Suddenly he tripped and dropped it.

"Geez, Bobby, can't you even hang on to a simple football?" his dad chided. "I swear, you haven't got a sports gene in your entire body."

Dana saw Bobby's expression fall and his shoulders slump. Steve gave him a hand up. "I'm calling it quits," Steve said. "Let's go inside, get Mom to make some popcorn."

"In a minute," Bobby said.

Their father threw his arm around Steve's shoulder and tugged him toward the house. "Come on, son. The game's starting."

Steve said to Bobby, "Coming?"

"In a minute. You go on."

Dana waited until Steve and his father had gone inside. She took Bobby's hand. "Come home with me and watch a movie. Who cares about TV football games?"

"Not today, Dana." He stood staring at the

back door of the house. "I know Dad wishes it was me who was sick instead of Steve."

"Don't say that."

"Why not? It's the truth." He shoved his hands into the pockets of his jacket. "And you know what? Sometimes I wish it was me too."

"Bobby, please . . ."

He faced her and she saw anger and pain in his eyes. "At least then I might not be invisible. I'm a stranger in my own house, Dana. Dad's mad at the world. All Mom does is cry. Nobody ever asks, 'So how are you doing, Bobby?' " He turned to Dana. "My brother's dying. My only brother and I can't even talk about it because it's too hard, because everybody hurts too much." Bobby struggled to regain control. "Yeah . . . I should be the one who's dying so I can get out of everybody's way."

"Stop it," she commanded. "I don't want you to die, Bobby."

"Who would miss me?"

"I would."

"Would you, Dana?"

She ignored his question. "And so would Steve. Do you really think he'd let you trade places with him?"

"Probably not." Bobby ground his fist into his other palm. "A reporter called a few days ago for an interview. Can you believe it? Steve's legend lives on in spite of everything."

"Steve's just a person, Bobby. Just a regular person that something terrible is happening to. Everybody's sorry."

His eyes looked haunted. "Are you the only person in the universe who isn't in love with my brother?"

She felt a chill go through her. "Why would you ask me that?"

"Because I think I'm going crazy. Sometimes I feel like you and I are a million miles apart, even when we're standing next to each other. Even when I'm kissing you."

Her stomach constricted. "Don't feel that way, Bobby. Please. This is hard on all of us."

He pulled her to him, and she put her arms around him, held him tightly. Over his shoulder, she saw Steve watching through the kitchen window.

Dana's piano teacher urged her to participate in a piano competition to be held in Atlanta right before Christmas, but Dana didn't want to go. "Why not?" the astounded Mrs. Sherrill asked. "This is a wonderful opportunity for you. Some of the best judges in the country will be there, as well as some of the top student talent in the Southeast. If you want a scholarship to Juilliard, I can't imagine a better testing ground."

Dana couldn't tell her teacher that she didn't want to leave Steve. Their time together was running out, and she couldn't waste any of it at a competition where she wouldn't be able to concentrate anyway. "My parents will send me to Juilliard with or without a scholarship," she told Mrs. Sherrill. "I can't go away right now. I just can't."

Her mother also urged Dana to go, but she wouldn't budge. "I thought becoming a concert pianist was your dream," her mother said. "You've always been so focused. What's wrong, Dana?"

"Dreams change," Dana answered.

"Please don't tell me you've gone off the deep end over Bobby. He's a nice guy and all, but don't throw away your future because of some high school crush."

Dana whirled and glared at her mother. "It isn't Bobby, Mom. Don't blame him. I'll compete in the state contest in the spring like I've always planned. If that gets me a scholarship, then good. If it doesn't, maybe I won't even go to Juilliard. There are other schools with good music programs, you know."

"Not go! But Dana, that's all you've talked about for years! What's happening to you?"

Tears welled in Dana's eyes. "Please don't yell at me, Mom. I—I can't take you yelling at me just now."

Her mother gave Dana a long, thoughtful look, then sighed, stepped forward, and hugged her. "I only want what you want. If Atlanta isn't something you want to do, then all right. But as to abandoning your plans to attend Juilliard, I will ask you to reconsider that. You're so close to having what you've always said you wanted. Don't get cold feet now, Dana. It's your dream and your future."

Dana nodded, grateful to have a mother who respected her decisions without giving her the third degree. "I—I won't let my dreams go, Mom," she said, sniffing back tears.

"I just may take a little bit longer getting them. Trust me."

For Christmas, Bobby gave Dana a necklace from which hung a gold heart embedded with a seed pearl. Steve gave her a book of poetry, a compilation of famous love poems stretching from ancient Greece to the present. "Remember when you read this, I'm a jock," Steve said with a sheepish grin. "I stood in the bookstore for over an hour trying to decide what book had the words I want to say to you. This one came the closest."

"I'll pretend you're reading them to me when I read it."

He closed his hand over hers. "Don't read it yet. Read it later . . . after I'm gone."

She knew what he meant and felt a heaviness inside her heart. His radiation treatments were over, and he'd been feeling pretty good throughout the holidays. She was thankful for the gift of time. "If that's what you want," she said.

"It's what I want."

She treasured both gifts. She showed off

Bobby's to friends and family and tucked Steve's away in her memory box, waiting for the day when she could no longer hear his voice or see his face to take it out and have him touch her through the words of long-dead poets and still-living ones.

In February, Steve's headaches returned with a vengeance, evidence that his tumor was on the move again. He lost his sense of taste, could no longer drive or leave the house. Dana was beside herself because now it was harder than ever to be alone with him.

She practiced relentlessly for the upcoming state competitions, driving herself to new levels of excellence. Bobby was her sole diversion. Their friends headed off to Florida for spring break. "I can't leave Steve," Bobby said. "Go if you want to."

"No," she said. "I don't want to. I wouldn't have a good time without you, knowing you were here alone." It was a partial truth. She couldn't leave Steve either.

In late March, SAT scores arrived for their high school. Dana scored high enough to meet Juilliard's academic standards, which pleased her parents and sealed their promise to send her there, scholarship or not. But Bobby Harrod earned 1600—a perfect score. He was one of only seven hundred high school seniors to do so in the entire country.

Nine

Bobby's SAT score brought him instant fame. The city newspaper called for an interview, and once the reporter picked up on Bobby's relationship to Steve, the great FSU quarterback struck down by cancer, other reporters came. "CNN showed the video clip from our local station last night," Bobby told Dana at school. "It about blew us away. We're all used to seeing Steve on the screen, not me. Dad didn't know what to say."

"Sorry I missed it. Did you like seeing yourself bragged about?"

He shrugged. "Face it, it's only news because I'm Steve's brother."

"No, it's news because only seven hundred other people in the country made a perfect score on their SATs."

A group of Bobby's friends walked past and made a ceremony of bowing toward him. "Knock it off, wise guys," Bobby said.

His friends laughed, but Dana could see that the attention pleased him. "So how should we celebrate your first national news coverage?" she asked.

"Celebrations will have to wait until after I get home from Brain Bowl."

Jackson High's team had advanced to the state finals, so Bobby and his teammates were headed off to Charlotte for the weekend.

"With you there, I'm sure we'll win," Dana told him. "And then we'll have two things to celebrate. The finals will be televised."

"On cable access," Bobby said dismissively. "But you will watch, won't you?"

"I wouldn't miss it. There's supposed to be a big party in the cafeteria with the whole school invited to watch. Maybe I'll have a seat of honor because I'm Bobby's girl." She grinned impishly.

"I want you to watch it at my house—with

Steve. He asked if that would be okay with me and I told him sure . . . that is, if it's okay with you, Dana."

She hadn't seen Steve in more than two weeks, and her heart leaped in anticipation. "It's okay with me," she said, hoping her voice didn't betray her eagerness.

"Steve doesn't see many people these days, so count yourself among the lucky few." Bobby adjusted his armload of books. "I want Steve to be happy, and if spending an afternoon with my girl will do the trick, I'm for it."

"Then your girl will be pleased to return the favor."

"I do it all for love," Bobby said, kissing her forehead.

She watched him walk away, ashamed of her deception but ecstatic about the opportunity to spend more time with the one she loved.

The Harrods had turned their family room into a hospital room just for Steve. He had a special bed, a TV, videos, and a laptop computer, as well as a table, sofa, and fireplace all to himself. Dana was impressed with the setup and told him so.

"I told Mom and Dad it wasn't necessary, but they insisted. I think they needed something to do, something else to think about." He gestured. "Besides, it's big enough for all of us to be together at the same time. No crowding." He held out his hand. "Come here. Let me look at you."

Her heart hammered. His illness was taking its toll. He was thinner, and his skin looked sallow. Gone were the tan and the thick muscles from hours of working out on the football field. His hair was growing back and his head was covered in a fine blond fuzz. "I've missed seeing you," she said, taking his hand. It felt light, as if his bones had gone hollow.

"Not as much as I've missed seeing you. Do you know what it's like to lie here day after day with nothing to do but think about us?"

"At least I've been able to keep busy with school."

He patted the edge of the bed. "Sit. Take the remote. We'd better find that cable show and watch Bobby shine."

She took the remote, flipped to the channel broadcasting the Bowl competition, and curled up in the bed next to Steve. "Where are your parents?"

"I asked them to watch the event with some of their friends, which they were happy to do. My moods haven't been the best these days. I really hate them hovering over me."

"They want to be close to you, Steve, for as long as possible. I know the feeling."

He studied her face. "Bobby's lucky to have you. I'd be hard-pressed to know what to do if—well, if things were different for me."

She would find it difficult too. She couldn't begin to wrap her mind around a life with no Steve at all.

The Brain Bowl started; she turned up the sound. "Bobby looks good on TV," she said.

"He's scared stiff," Steve said. "I can tell by the way he's clenching his jaw."

Knowing Bobby's habit too, Dana smiled. "He does it when he's scared or anxious."

They watched as Bobby's team fired off correct answers and pulled ahead of its opponents. Bobby answered many of the questions himself, doing complicated math equations in his head. "He's so smart," Steve said when the competition took a station break. "It blows me away."

"And you're so athletic," Dana said.

"Too bad we didn't each get a little of what the other had."

"No, it isn't. Then you'd both be just average instead of brilliant in two separate ways."

Steve squeezed her hand. "You're brilliant too. I wish I could listen to you play the piano. It helps, you know, when I hurt really bad."

She was touched. "I'll make you some tapes."

"Not as good as the real thing, but that'll have to do. I wish I could hear you play in April."

"Don't worry—my parents will videotape the whole thing. You'll see the performance."

He toyed with a strand of her hair. "When this is over for me—"

"Don't talk that way."

"Dana, it's going to be over." Tears welled in her eyes, and he wiped them with his fingertip. "I want you to know that without you, I'd never have made it this long."

She opened her mouth to speak, but he

shushed her. "Thank you for loving me, Dana. Thank you with all my heart."

She held him, pressing her face into his chest. In the background, she heard the Brain Bowl commentator declare her high school's team the winner. She heard Steve say, "Way to go, Bobby!" She knew Bobby would be giving his teammates high fives and holding the trophy up to the camera. She knew all these things but couldn't look because being held by Steve was the sum total of her existence at that moment. She kissed him and was consumed by the eerie sensation that she would not be alone with him again, that this would be their last kiss.

Bobby came home a hero. The principal ordered a pep rally in the gym, where the Brain Bowl team was treated to an hour of skits by classmates and praise from the faculty. Dana sat in the bleachers and cheered along with Bobby's parents, who'd been invited for the celebration. Steve arrived in a wheelchair, and Bobby made a speech saying that it was Steve's example of excellence that had always spurred him on. Dana did not make eye contact with

Steve because she knew she could not have kept from sobbing uncontrollably.

The silver trophy was placed in the glass case usually reserved for athletic awards next to the principal's office. Bobby's name was engraved ahead of the others on the trophy because he'd been the team captain. The same afternoon, Bobby received a scholarship offer from Cal Tech. "Can you believe it?" he shouted to Dana over the phone. "They're offering me a *full* ride, Dana. All expenses paid as long as I maintain a B-plus average."

"No problem," she said.

"Even my old man's impressed."

"I'm happy for you, Bobby. You deserve the best."

"I already have the best," he said. "I have you."

She felt a stab of guilt. "Take the scholarship."

"That's what Steve told me to do too. But I can't leave until—well, until."

Until Steve is gone, Dana finished in her mind. *Neither of us can.*

At six the next morning, Dana's phone rang. She grabbed the receiver, her heart pounding because she knew it would not be good news. "Yes," she said, holding her breath.

"It's me." Bobby's voice cracked. "The paramedics just left." There was a long pause. "Steve died in his sleep during the night. They said he had a stroke and that he went without pain. That's a good thing, isn't it?"

Dana's throat had closed up and she couldn't speak.

"My brother's dead, Dana. What are we going to do without him?"

Ten

∿

The humid heat of late August settled around Dana, and the scent of the last of her mother's blooming roses drifted in the air. She sat on her front porch reading the book of poetry Steve had given her for Christmas. Four months had passed since his death—four months, three weeks, and two days. She had missed him on every single one of those days. She smoothed her hand across the page of the poem Steve had marked as his favorite, "How Do I Love Thee." She'd read it so many times that she could recite it from memory. It would always be her favorite too.

In another week, she would leave for New

York and for Juilliard. She hadn't gotten a scholarship in the spring. She'd played well in the state competitions, walking away with Superiors and Excellents from the judges, but it hadn't been enough. Still, she was going to the college that it had been her lifelong dream to attend, and her parents were happy because they believed she was happy. She *was*, in a way, but she also knew that Juilliard was never going to hold the importance it had once held for her. Her life had been forever changed by a love she'd experienced for a man who'd died. The poem spoke eloquently of all she felt.

She heard the crunch of tires in her driveway and looked up to see Bobby getting out of his car. Quickly she tucked the book beneath the cushion on the porch swing and rose to welcome him. "How's it going?" she asked. "All packed?"

"All packed." He came onto the porch, kissed her lightly, and returned with her to the swing. "The trailer is full, and Dad's raring to go. I still can't believe we're driving all the way to California together." He rolled his eyes. "Six whole days in a car with Dad. It's going to seem like forever."

"You'll talk."

"About what? Ever since Steve—" Bobby interrupted himself. "I know Dad's trying, but we don't have too much in common."

"You have Steve. And your dad's proud of you, Bobby. I think he's trying to make up for lost years."

Bobby grinned. "You still work hard to make everything right and everybody happy, don't you, Dana?"

"Old habit, I guess."

They had finished the school year as a couple, but things were not the same between them. Dana realized that she had created the sense of distance, but there was nothing she could do about it. Luckily, Bobby had been busy. He'd gotten a job as soon as school was out to earn spending money for college. He came by now and then, even took her out occasionally. To her surprise, he hadn't griped or complained about their lack of togetherness, just made himself available if she wanted to be with him. Winning the scholarship had gone a long way toward building his self-confidence; he seemed more at peace, more self-assured and settled. She was glad about that.

"Do you want some lemonade? There's a pitcher in the kitchen—"

"No, I can't stay. Dad wants to head out early. I came to say goodbye."

The very word hit her hard and caused her eyes to mist over.

"Hey, those aren't for me, are they?"

She shrugged. "Maybe for a lot of things."

"I'll see you at Christmas when I come home."

"I'm doing a short concert tour at Christmas," Dana said. "We'll be in Europe."

Bobby looked resigned. "Then maybe next summer."

She nodded. He stood and so did she. He took her by the elbows and gazed deeply into her eyes. "One of the reasons I came over tonight was to thank you."

"For what?"

"For being my girl this past year. It meant everything to have you stick by me ... through Steve and all. I know you didn't have to, that you could have cut out, but you didn't."

The truth sprang to her lips. She should tell him about her and Steve. Except that she knew

it would serve no good purpose except to un-
burden her conscience. It would hurt Bobby,
and hadn't it been her goal from the very beginning to *not* hurt Bobby? He'd been hurt
enough by the loss of his brother. She swallowed the truth. "You made it easy for me,"
she said.

"Because I'm so adorable?" he asked, mis-
chief twinkling in his eyes.

"Totally adorable."

"I love you," he said, growing serious.

She couldn't say those words to him, not
now, so she rose on her toes and kissed him.
"You take care of yourself. Write me, you
hear? Tell me all about sunny California."

"And you write me about New York. I may
never get there myself." He slipped his hand
into his back pocket and pulled out a partly
crumpled envelope. "Read this after I'm out of
here, and know that I mean every word of it."

She took the sealed envelope, then watched
him spring down the porch steps and get into
his car. He waved as he backed out of her
driveway. Returning to the swing, she tore
open the envelope. In the fading evening light,
she read his message. Her breath caught. Her

heart tripped a beat. She jumped up and ran to the edge of the porch in time to see his tail-lights disappear around the corner.

Trembling, Dana pressed Bobby's letter against her breast. She gathered her composure and read it again.

Dearest Dana,

You taught me that real love is special, a gift from the heart, even when the heart belongs to another. Yes, I knew about you and Steve. There was no way either of you could hide your feelings from me. It was written on your faces every time you looked at each other. I was hurt, something I know both of you tried to avoid. But when I thought about it, really thought about it, I realized that let-ting you and Steve be together and keeping my mouth shut *was the one thing of true value I could give him as he faced the end of his life.*

It was a very hard thing to do, and there will be people who think that I should hate you for deceiving me. I only wish I could. But I can't. For I've learned that you often don't get to choose who you love. Love happens

*when you're not even looking for it. It was
that way for me when I met you. It was that
way for my brother. We both loved you, and I
honestly believe that you loved both of us.
Just differently.*

Tears blurred Dana's vision. All the while
she had thought she was protecting Bobby,
when in actuality it had been the other way
around. And yes, Bobby was correct, she had
loved them both.

Dana felt the lifting of her own sense of
guilt, and she wondered which of them had
given the other one the greater gift. She
couldn't say. All she knew was that she felt
honored to have been Bobby's girl. She would
tell him that one day when the pain might not
be so fresh for either of them.

She held up the letter to read the final sen-
tences, written in Bobby's neat, precise hand-
writing.

*I don't have words to tell you exactly how
I feel, so I'll write the words I read in a book
I saw in Steve's hands last Christmas. He
had fallen asleep with the book propped on*

his chest. I lifted it, read it, and knew that just like Steve . . .

> "*I love thee with the breath,*
> *Smiles, tears, of all my life!—and, if God choose,*
> *I shall but love thee better after death.*"

BOOK THREE

Laura's Heart

One

She couldn't breathe. Gasping for air, Laura Carson struggled to keep from blacking out and not to panic. It wasn't as if this hadn't happened many times before. Above her, she saw the faces of emergency room doctors and nurses. Behind them, she saw her anxious parents.

"We got her here as fast as we could," her mother told one of the doctors. "It came on so suddenly. We didn't have any warning."

"Yes, Mrs. Carson. We're doing all we can for Laura."

A doctor eased an oxygen mask over Laura's face. A nurse shot a syringeful of medication into the IV line already hooked to her arm. Immediately Laura felt her breathing slow, her heart stop its awful fluttering. Electrodes were stuck onto her heaving chest and hooked to a bedside heart monitor. The green squiggly line looked like an electronic scream. Laura knew that in a way it was a scream—a cry for help from her virus-damaged heart. She should be used to it. It had been going on for four years, this failing of her heart, this struggling, stutter-step dance it did when she least expected it. She also knew she'd never get used to it.

"How are we feeling, Laura?" The doctor leaned over her.

His face came into focus slowly. Why did doctors always speak in the first person plural? As if they were victims too? This doctor wasn't. He couldn't possibly know what it was like to live like a broken toy, never knowing when she'd wind down. "I'm . . . fine," she managed to say.

"She's not fine," her father contradicted. "I want her heart specialist called immediately."

"Dr. Simon's already been paged. She should be here soon."

As if she'd heard her name, Dr. Simon breezed into the room. She was a tall, slender woman in her forties, with salt-and-pepper hair pulled back in a severe bun. She wore no makeup. "What's up?" she asked the ER doctor.

He rattled off a list of medical terms, which Laura ignored. *My heart's lousy*, Laura wanted to say sarcastically. *And you-all can't fix it.* The muscle, weakened by a virus when she was twelve, had turned her into an invalid, and there didn't seem to be anything medical science could do to change it for her.

"Look, Laura, I'm going to have to admit you," Dr. Simon said, looking down at her.

"No—" Laura gasped, trying to pull off the oxygen mask.

Dr. Simon held down Laura's hand. "I know it's not what you want, but we have no choice."

"School—"

"Can wait," the doctor said firmly.

"I . . . just started back . . ." Tears welled in Laura's eyes.

"I know. But there's no choice. You've got pneumonia in your left lung, and that's making your heart work harder. We all know it *can't* work harder." Dr. Simon's voice was soft and kind, but the blow it delivered to Laura felt devastating.

"How long this time?" Laura asked, blinking back tears. Over the past year, she'd spent a total of six weeks in the hospital. Now, here at the start of the final two months of her junior year, she was going to have to drop out of classes once more. It wasn't fair.

"As long as it takes," Dr. Simon answered.

Laura's mother took her hand. "I'll get your teachers to prepare work for you. You'll be able to keep up."

"Keeping up isn't the problem," Laura said. How did she explain that her long absences from school made her a social outcast? Cliques were set. Friends were bonded. Boys had already chosen girlfriends and dates to the junior-senior dance. Laura only had one true friend—Bonnie Tyler—and with this newest sentence of hospital imprisonment, she had little hope of fitting in again.

"I'm sorry, honey."

Laura nodded, resigned. She had no arguments left. She was going to be hospitalized regardless. Arguments and tears took breath and energy, and at the moment, she had neither.

Laura's room in the teen wing of the hospital's pediatric floor was private and overlooked the Hudson River. The trees lining the river's banks were just beginning to emerge from their winter's sleep, and their branches appeared to be trimmed with green lace. "Nice view," Laura's father said. "I'll get an orderly to push your bed closer to the window so you can enjoy it."

The staff had welcomed her when she'd come on the floor. Most knew her name, as she knew theirs. Not much turnover, which her father always said was a sign of employee contentment. He ran his own small computer business and employed several workers. But Laura didn't care about nurses loving their jobs—she just liked seeing familiar faces.

A nurse named Betsy set up an oxygen tent above Laura's bed. "We'll get these vapors going and you'll feel better in no time," Betsy said.

"Not soon enough." Laura knew the drill by heart: Oxygen tent until her lungs cleared.

Meds in her IV lines to heal her lungs and calm her heart. When she came out of the tent, more days in bed hooked to oxygen. Then, slowly, she could get up and venture down the hall in a wheelchair to the game room. Finally she could begin walking. And then one day, when Dr. Simon deemed it all right, she could go home. Until the next time. And there was always a next time.

Her father asked about moving the bed.

"I'll have to get longer tubing," Betsy said. The oxygen hookup came out of the wall above Laura's bed. "But it shouldn't be a problem. I'll have someone come up and position the bed later." She patted Laura's arm. "Nothing's too good for one of my favorite patients."

Laura said, "Thank you."

"You should get some sleep," her father said.

"Yes, honey," her mother concurred. "Sleep now. Let the medications do their job. We'll come back this evening."

"Call Bonnie for me. She'll be wondering why I'm not in school."

"I'll let her know," Laura's mother said.

Through the plastic film of the oxygen tent,

Laura watched her parents leave, wishing she could go home with them. The oxygen made a faint hissing sound, and soon her eyelids felt heavy. She wanted to sleep and wake up when this nightmare was over. She wanted a healthy heart. She wanted to be normal. She wanted to ride her horse on their farm in upstate New York. Laura Carson wanted her life back.

Laura dreamed that she was adrift in a boat on the Hudson River. She lay stretched out on a pallet of spring flowers, her long blond hair trailing onto the floor planks like the Lady of Shalott in a poem she'd read in English class. She was a petal floating on calm water, lazy, at peace, and free of pain. From the far bank, she heard soft, sultry guitar music. Laura tried to raise her head and search for the musician but couldn't. It was as if she were tied to the pallet, unable to move. Her heart, her poor, sad heart, began to pound crazily.

She woke with a start, only to realize that her hospital bed was actually moving. She let out a cry. The bed stopped. A male face peered through the plastic film of her oxygen tent. Even through the distortion of the plastic, she saw that he was Latino, his face strong boned, his eyes dark brown, and his hair thick and black.

"Forgive me for waking you," he said. "I thought I could move your bed to the window while you slept. I did not mean to frighten you, Sleeping Beauty."

Two

~

"**W**ho are you?" Laura asked. The head of the bed was elevated because it was easier for her to breathe and rest in an upright position.

His face broke into a heart-stopping smile. "I am Ramon Ochoa—at your service. I work the four-to-midnight shift as an orderly. You would not remember me because I was but a janitor when you were last here. But I remember you—the beautiful girl with the heart like paper."

She felt a self-conscious jolt. So she was the girl with the paper heart to him. Ramon wore green hospital scrubs. An earplug was tethered to the pocket in the center of his chest. "I was dreaming," she said. "I heard pretty music."

Quickly he reached into his pocket, and the music faded. "I listen to classical guitar music while I work."

"You don't have to turn it off."

"Later," he said with another smile. "I'm sorry you are sick and in the hospital again, Laura."

He said her name with familiarity, as if they were old friends, and she found it strangely exciting. "I'm sorry too. I was hoping I wouldn't have to come back . . . especially so soon."

"I don't like to see you sad. Maybe when you wake in the morning the sun will be shining on the river. That's why I moved your bed while you were sleeping, to surprise you with the sunrise. Except I woke you instead. For that, I am also sorry."

"I don't mind. Really. Sleeping is all I have to do. Sleep and dream. I was dreaming that I was floating on the river in a boat." She didn't know why she told him that, except that she was fully awake and didn't want to be alone. Plus, she liked hearing him talk, the slight Spanish accent, the lyrical rhythm of his voice.

"And what happened in your dream?"

"Nothing . . . it was dumb." She didn't want to admit that she'd seen herself as a dead medieval princess.

"Dreams are never dumb. They are our fears and our deepest wishes. They tell us about ourselves."

She wondered if she was afraid. Or was she longing for peace and serenity such as she'd felt in the dream? "So you only came into the room to move my bed?" she asked.

"When this room is empty, I come and stand at the window and look down at the river. I think the water has stories to tell. And secrets."

"What kind of secrets?"

"The secrets belong to the river."

"Do you live near the river?"

"I live very far from it, but I have gone down and walked in the woods alongside the river many times."

"Has it told you any stories?"

"A few."

"Like what?"

He laughed. "You should be a lawyer. You ask so many questions."

"What has it told you?"

Ramon leaned closer. "It has told me that if I do not return to doing my job, I will no longer be working at the hospital."

She made a face. "That's sneaky. You just don't want to tell me. It's not like I can go down and listen to the river myself, you know."

"That's true." He glanced over his shoulder. "Perhaps I will tell you later."

"When?"

"You would like me to visit you again?" He looked surprised.

"Yes." She meant it because he intrigued her.

"But you will be asleep when I get off work."

"Then tomorrow."

He studied her face through the plastic tent, making her heart beat faster.

"I take my dinner break at nine."

"Eat fast, then come see me. Check first to see if I'm alone." She figured her parents would visit her every evening, but because they both worked at her father's store, they went home by nine-thirty.

"If that is what you want, I will come."

"And you'll tell me the river's secrets?"

"Only if you'll tell me your dream."

"A deal." She watched him back away. "I'm glad I woke up," she said, suddenly dreading being alone. Nights in the hospital seemed extra long.

"I hope you will get back to sleep quickly."

"It was the music, I think. The guitar sounded sad. And lonely. Like me."

He pulled the minidisc player out of his pocket and the plug from his ear. "Listen some more, if you like."

"I can't take your disc player."

He pressed it into her hand just outside the tent. "I'll return for it tomorrow."

She watched him duck out the door. In the quiet he left behind, she could hear the swish of her blood in her ears, the beep of the heart monitor beside her bed, the hiss of oxygen coming through the tubing. Talking to him had made it easy to forget how sick she was. She picked up the minidisc player, pulled it inside the tent, and put it against her cheek. It was still warm from his body.

Bonnie came to visit the next afternoon, and Laura told her about Ramon.

"Lucky you," Bonnie said. "I mean about

meeting a cute guy, not about being back in the hospital."

"I guess without the one I wouldn't have had the other."

"True, but I wish you were back at school. Bill asked Joanie Elkhart to the junior-senior dance."

Laura felt a wave of dismay. She'd been hoping Bill Southlund would ask her. "Well, there goes that dream," she said. "How about you? Did Tony ask you?"

"Not yet, but I heard he was going to."

Laura realized that once again life was passing her by, leaving her with the wreckage of dreams and plans for a life she couldn't quite live because of her bad heart. She reached out and squeezed Bonnie's hand. "If he doesn't, you ask him. You're a junior too, and you can invite him just as easily."

Bonnie chewed her lower lip. "You think that would be all right? Because the suspense is killing me between wishing he would and being afraid he won't. Even if he says no, I won't be sitting around chewing my nails."

"I would ask him if I were you. Life's short."

"Oh, Laura . . . I didn't mean—"

"To make me feel bad? It's okay. I know my life's never going to be normal. Every time I think things will be all right, I get sick. It's just the way things are, Bonnie. I'm getting used to it."

"Well, I think your doctors should come up with some plan to fix you up. Why'd they go to medical school in the first place?"

Laura sighed. "To hook me up to oxygen and heart monitors, I think."

"Bad doctors," Bonnie said, as if scolding a puppy.

"Not bad," Laura said. "Just out of options."

When Bonnie left, Laura turned toward the window and her view of the river below. In truth, she only had one option left, but that one was so scary that she could hardly stand to think about it. She looked at her bedside clock. In only a few more hours Ramon would return. "You will come, won't you?" she said to herself. *Please come. Please.*

Three

By nine-thirty that night, Ramon had still not come to see Laura. She kept his disc player under her pillow and listened to the plaintive strains of the haunting classical guitar music until she got a lump in her throat and felt as if she'd cry from the sheer beauty of it. When her mother had seen Laura with the player earlier, she'd asked, "Where did that come from?"

"I borrowed it from a friend."

"It was thoughtful of Bonnie to bring it," her mother said, making an assumption Laura didn't bother to correct. "But your father and I can buy you one of your own. All you have to do is ask."

"I like this one."

"Why? I'm certain we can buy a better one. I'll research the different brands, and we can stop at an audio store tomorrow—"

"This one is fine, Mom."

"But if you like it so much, why wouldn't you want one of your own?"

Because if you buy me one, I have no reason to hold on to Ramon's, she thought. "Mom, I don't have to own everything," she insisted. "I just like borrowing things once in a while. It makes me feel like someone expects me to live long enough to give them back."

Her mother hadn't mentioned it again, and now, as the hospital quieted down for the night, Laura began to doubt that Ramon would come to retrieve his disc player at all. He probably had a bagful and went from room to room giving them out to lonely girls trapped in hospital beds.

"I'm sorry I'm late, Laura." Ramon ducked inside her room after ten o'clock. "I had to clean an operating room."

All her dark thoughts vanished at the sight of him. "I wasn't worried," she fibbed. "Plus I had your disc player. I figured you'd come back for it."

He came to her bedside. "The player is nothing. It is you I want to see."

Her feelings of rejection did an about-face. "Thank you for letting me borrow the player. I love the music."

He reached into his pocket and withdrew several minidiscs. "Here are others."

"But it's your player, and I should give it back. My parents will buy me my own."

Ramon grinned. "Then you will have no reason to let me visit."

She returned his smile, touched that they'd shared the same thought. "You don't need a reason."

He placed the discs in her hand. "I can't stay. I have work to do, but I could not begin again without seeing you first."

"Will you promise to come back tonight?"

His eyes clouded. "I don't know . . . Your doctor wants you to rest."

"I rest all day."

"It would be very late, and the nurse on duty—"

"I don't care. The nurse takes vitals at twelve and three. You can visit between her rounds. Please. I'm lonely here."

His expression softened. "I can deny you nothing, Laura. Spending time with you is my greatest wish. I never thought you'd consider spending time with someone like me."

"What's wrong with you?"

He shrugged. "I am only an orderly."

"So? Is that what you'll always be?"

"I'd like to go to medical school one day. I'd like to become a doctor."

"Who takes care of girls with paper hearts?"

"Who takes care of girls with beautiful hearts?"

He said such wonderful things to her, unlike the boys in her classes. She'd had crushes on several, but they all seemed to be very much into their own lives—friends, sports, cars. If any of them had had a crush on her, it was a well-kept secret. "I should be out of this tent in a few days. I'll be mobile soon. Maybe we could go down to the rec room together."

"I have another job. I leave this one, go home, sleep, get up, and work at a grocery store in my neighborhood until it is time for me to leave for this job."

Her heart sank. "I—I didn't mean to get carried away. Of course you have a life, and if you work until midnight, this must be the last place you'd want to be in the daytime."

He leaned closer, his eyes full of emotion. "I will cut back my hours at the grocery store if it means I can spend more time with you."

"You'd do that for me?"

"I'd do most anything for you."

"But why? You hardly know me."

"I have seen you come since I began my job here. There was something about you that touched my heart. I know that doesn't make sense to you, but it does to me. People do not choose how they feel about someone. You just one day see that special person, and your heart reacts. Your soul jumps up and you think, 'I've waited all my life to meet this person.' It has been that way for me, Laura. From the time I first saw you, I cared for you."

She was shocked speechless.

Ramon took a step backward. "I have said too much, haven't I? Forgive me. I didn't mean to push myself on you."

"No one's ever said anything like that to me before." No one had ever confessed to adoring her, especially since her heart had gone bad. Few guys seemed even to want to be around an invalid. "I think I like hearing it," she added shyly.

His smile lit up his face. "I have wanted to tell you every time you came into the hospital how I felt, but I did not know you, and until last night I had little hope of meeting you. I expect nothing from you, Laura. You may never feel for me as I do for you, and that's all right."

"There's not much I can give back to you, Ramon. But if you'll visit me, you know, give me your time, well, I'd like that a lot."

Their gazes locked and held. Laura felt her insides turn to jelly.

"I'll come tomorrow afternoon early, before my shift begins," he said. "Is that okay?"

"Totally okay." The air felt charged. She held out her hand and he brushed his fingers across her palm, sending shivers up her spine.

"Until tomorrow," Ramon said.

"Are you positive you don't want your disc player back?" she asked.

"It's not needed. Now I have music in my heart." He slipped out of her room.

Ramon kept his promise. He came in an hour early the next day and every day that week to stay with Laura. She discovered that he was good medicine. By the end of the week, she was out of the oxygen tent and able to move around her room on her own.

"I'm amazed by your progress," Dr. Simon said.

"Is my heart better?" Laura wanted to know.

"Your heart will never be better, Laura. You know that. But the pneumonia has cleared quickly, which puts less strain on your heart, and that's a good thing." The doctor wrote notes on her chart, finishing minutes later and giving Laura a quizzical look. "I've just told you you're better, and you haven't bombarded me with pleas to go home and back to school. Don't tell me you're starting to like it here."

"It's not so bad. This time, I mean. I don't mind staying awhile longer." Laura didn't meet the doctor's gaze as she answered, afraid she'd be asked more questions.

"That's good, because I want to keep you here a few more days. Run some tests."

"If you say so."

Dr. Simon smiled. "That's what I like—a

cooperative patient. Now be a good girl and get back into bed for me."

Laura glanced anxiously at the clock. Dr. Simon had stayed well into Ramon's visiting time, and Laura was eager for her to hurry on her way. The doctor's beeper went off, and once she'd gone, Ramon stepped into the room, shutting the door behind him.

"I didn't think she'd ever leave," Laura said as he pulled a chair closer to her.

"She's your doctor. What did she say to you?"

"More tests. But that means I'll be around longer. What do you think of that?"

He grinned. "I have been dreading the time when you will be leaving. I'll miss you."

"You don't have to miss me. You can come see me at home."

His smile faded. He leaned forward, took her hand, and pressed her palm against his broad chest. She felt his heartbeat strong and steady through the fabric of his clothing. "That wouldn't be possible, Laura."

"But why? I thought you liked me."

He didn't get to answer. Just then, her

mother swooped into her room, saying, "Surprise! I got off work early and—" She stopped short when she saw Ramon. "What's going on here?" she asked, her eyes narrowing suspiciously. "Who are you? And why are you in Laura's room holding her hand?"

Four

Ramon stood so quickly that his chair tipped backward. "Forgive me, Mrs. Carson."

"Mom! Don't yell at Ramon. He's a friend."

Laura's mother's gaze was frosty and swept over Ramon from head to toe. "So I can see."

He dropped Laura's hand as if he'd been burned. "I work here, and I visit with Laura whenever I can. Please don't be angry—"

"I'll be what ever I want to be." Laura's mother cut him off. "I think you'd better leave now. Who's your supervisor, anyway?"

"Mom, stop it!" Laura said.

"It's all right," Ramon said. "I will leave."

He exited the room quickly, and Laura turned on her mother. "Well, thank you very much! I can't believe how rude you were to him."

"And I can't believe I walked into your room—a bedroom, I might add—and found you holding hands with some man who's part of the hired help. What were you thinking?"

"I was thinking that Ramon is one of the nicest people I've ever met and you just ran him off."

"Nice? How nice can he be if you didn't even bother to mention him to your father and me? Has he been meeting with you long? I won't tolerate it, Laura. I won't."

Laura felt ill. Her heart had begun to thud, sending spikes along the screen of the monitor. Within seconds, Betsy rushed into the room. "Are you all right?" she asked. "Your monitor's going crazy."

Laura couldn't catch her breath.

"I'll call your doctor."

"No . . . ," she managed to say. "She was just . . . here. I need to . . . get in bed."

Betsy helped her while her mother stood

aside, her face looking pinched and white. "I—it's my fault," Karen Carson said. "I got her agitated."

Betsy settled Laura, slipped the oxygen tubing into her nose, and took her pulse. "She's calming down," Betsy said. "I'm calling Dr. Simon."

"Yes, please," Laura's mother said. "This is my fault. I'm so sorry," she told Laura when Betsy had gone.

"Yes, it is," Laura said, angry enough to let her mother take the blame. "You had no right to be so mean to Ramon. He's very nice, and he's made this hospital stay bearable for me. Don't you understand what it's like to be completely cut off from the normal world? I can't go to school. I can't do anything. It's my junior year, Mom, and I can't even sit in a classroom."

"We've tried to make it better for you. Your father and I were going to tell you this together, but I think you need to hear it now. He's gotten permission from the school superintendent to set up Minicams in your classrooms. You can attend classes from your own bedroom at home. You can participate in the class, even ask questions and be called upon. Isn't that wonderful? You'll be there, but still perfectly safe at home."

Laura was horrified. Now she had one more thing that set her apart from the real world— she was going to be placed in a bubble, a freak who viewed life through a TV monitor. "No," she said. "It's creepy."

Her mother looked puzzled. "But why? We thought this would please you. You're always talking about attending classes—"

"That's right. *Attending* classes. Not watching life pass me by."

"Laura, I just don't understand you."

"I know," she said. The discussion had exhausted her, and she sank into the pillows.

Betsy came in with a medicine cup. "Dr. Simon wants you to take this. It'll relax you."

Laura didn't want any pill, but she was out of energy, too tired to argue. She took the pill, shut her eyes, and concentrated on seeing Ramon's face. Not the frightened face he'd shown when her mother had confronted him, but the smiling, gentle, adoring face he wore during their long conversations. She drifted to sleep dreaming of his beautiful brown eyes gazing at her.

Laura awoke in the dark and saw Ramon sitting beside her bed. "You came back." Her voice was a hoarse whisper. "I'm so glad."

"Don't talk," he said, taking her hand and kissing her palm tenderly.

"What . . . time?" Her tongue felt thick, and her brain was foggy.

"It's after midnight. I have finished my shift, but I could not leave without seeing you."

"I'm sorry . . . about my . . . mother."

He shrugged. "She is a mother. My presence upset her. Don't think about it. Just rest."

"She had . . . no right . . ."

"I'm a stranger. She walked in and I'm holding your hand. I understand her feelings and I don't judge her. She loves you."

"She's . . . smothering me. Ever since I've been . . . sick, my parents are all over me. They make me . . . crazy."

"You are lucky to have ones who care so much for you."

The way he said it made her wonder about his life at home. How had he grown up? Had his parents been uncaring? She would have asked, except the pill Betsy had given her earlier was dragging her back toward oblivion. "Please say you'll come again," she managed to say.

He laced his fingers through hers. "Don't you know? Nothing can keep me from you, Laura. Not even angry mothers."

"Mom told me you were upset about the cameras in your classrooms, honey. You know that's not what we intended. We really thought it would be easier for you to participate, that's all." Laura's father was visiting the next afternoon when he broached the topic of the Minicams.

She sat at the table, looking out at the river winding like a long golden ribbon in the rays of the setting sun. "I overreacted. It caught me off guard, but I've had time to think about it and it's not such a terrible idea. Really." She had decided against arguing. Ramon had been right—they had only meant to help her.

"That's good." Her father looked relieved. "Actually, the superintendent said it could act as some sort of pilot program for homebound teaching. It could make the classroom more accessible, keep kids more a part of school life."

"I guess it's okay if I don't have a camera aimed back at me."

"Only if you want one. Your teachers said they'd welcome a monitor in their rooms if you were the star." He winked. "You could see everybody, and everybody could see you."

"Maybe later." She hedged. Some days she didn't have the strength to sit up in bed and couldn't imagine a roomful of classmates watching her answer questions.

"It's the next best thing to being there," her father said. "State of the art. Twenty-first-century stuff. Cutting edge."

He was trying so hard that she had to smile. "I said it was all right to put cameras in my classrooms. Besides, this way I might be able to see what Doug Harris and his jock friends actually *do* during class. It isn't studying."

Her dad smiled. "That's my girl. And it's temporary. As soon as the doc says you can go back to classes, the cameras go dark."

"Maybe it's better this way. I won't have to think about what to wear every day. You guys have no idea how hard that can be."

His smile faded as he sat straighter and cleared his throat. "I don't want to upset you like Mom did, but we have to talk about the young man who came to your room."

She took a deep breath, knowing that sooner or later it would have to be discussed. "What about Ramon?"

"He's twenty-one, Laura."

She hadn't known he was that old, but she kept her face expressionless. "So?"

"So, you're sixteen. That's a big age gap. Even if you were without a single health problem, we wouldn't let you see a guy that old."

"He's not ancient, Daddy. And we're just friends. He's going to be a doctor someday."

"Is that what he told you?"

"Yes. He has goals, and he works here. I don't see what the big deal's all about."

Her father sat quietly, as if weighing his words. "Did he also tell you that he's a criminal? That he's been in and out of trouble with the law since he was eleven? That he's spent four years in a juvenile detention center? And that he once headed up one of most terrifying youth gangs in the city?"

Five

Laura had not known any of those things about Ramon, but she was careful to hide her shock. "I told you we were friends, Dad. I know what I need to know about him."

"Then you must also know that he's not the kind of boy we want hanging around you. He's bad news, Laura. Stay away from him."

She held her tongue, knowing it was useless to argue, but she didn't like the way he was ordering her around, as if she were some kind of baby who had to be told what to do. She was also so shaken by the information that she wanted time to sort out her emotions. "I think

I owe him the courtesy of telling him to his face, don't you?"

"I'm not so sure—"

"Please. He's been nice to me. I can't just cut him off."

Her father weighed her request. "I guess that would be all right. Does he make it a habit of dropping by every day? I'll get the nurses to keep him out once you've talked to him."

"I can handle it, Dad. Please don't bring anybody else into it."

"All right. But I mean it, Laura. I don't want him coming round again. You've got enough to think about just getting well and coming home. And speaking of home, Dr. Simon thinks she'll release you either tomorrow or the next day. Isn't that good news?"

"Yes, Dad. It's good news," Laura said, her mind still reeling. Ramon had lied to her. *Why?*

By the time Ramon showed up that night, Laura was sick with apprehension. She felt duped, betrayed. They'd had numerous conversations, flights of fancy really, where she'd told him her dreams and hopes about getting well via some miraculous new drug, going to art school, hiking the Appalachian Trail, and having her own pottery studio one day. And he'd told her how he wanted to be a doctor, opening a clinic in the city's poorest communities to take care of children who had no other health care. She had believed him. Without question. Now she wondered if he'd only been feeding her a line. Why would he have kept his past such a secret?

She told him exactly what her father had said, never once taking her gaze off his face as she spoke. "Is it true, Ramon?" she asked when she was finished. "Is all that true?"

His eyes had grown dark, and his mouth was set in a grim line. "All of it is true."

She felt as if he'd slapped her. "Why didn't you tell me? Why did you lie to me?"

"I did not lie."

"But you didn't tell me the truth either. The only thing you ever said to me was that it would be impossible for us to see each other once I got out of the hospital."

"I was ashamed of my old life. I didn't want you to know. How was I to bring it up when I want so much to leave that old life behind me? When I'm trying so hard to forget who I once was and focus now on who I want to be? Would you have still been my friend, Laura? Would you have talked to me, shared your heart with me, if you had known about the other Ramon?"

She saw anguish etched in his face, and she felt sorry for him. And for herself. "I don't know," she answered truthfully. "But then I never had the chance, did I?"

He stood. "I will go. And I will not bother you again."

Her heart lurched. She didn't want him to go, but her feelings about him were in turmoil. "My parents don't want me to see you anymore. I'm afraid that if I do they'll make trouble for you. I don't want you to lose your job."

"I'm used to trouble. It's followed me all my life." He crossed to the door, turned. "Did you like me, Laura? Even just a little? Please, be honest."

She nodded, not trusting her voice.

"I still care about you, you know. And I thank you with all my heart for the time we've spent together. Seeing you every day, talking to you, just being in the same room with you has been the best part of my days. You may find that hard to believe, but it is the truth. And that is what you want from me, isn't it? The truth?"

Once he was gone, she returned to her bed, buried her face in a pillow, and wept.

"You're just going to let your parents tell you who you can see and who you can't?" Bonnie had come for a visit on Saturday morning, and after hearing Laura's tearful story about Ramon, she'd fired off her question.

"Don't you think I'm dying inside about this?"

"But why is it so terrible for you to see him? I mean, you're stuck here in the hospital. What horrible thing is he going to do to you?"

"Ramon would never hurt me. Maybe he's done bad things in the past, but he's not a criminal now. He's trying really hard to make something of himself. He works hard. He has plans for a future."

"Hey, you don't have to convince me. It's your parents you have to persuade."

The more Laura thought about it, the madder she got. What right did her parents have to pass judgment on Ramon without ever getting to know him? It wasn't fair. He'd treated Laura with great respect. He was kinder to her than any boy had ever been, nicer, more respectful. "I don't know what to do," Laura confessed to her friend.

"If it were me, I'd at least tell him how you feel."

Going against her parent's wishes seemed foreign to Laura. She'd never lied to them. "I don't want Mom and Dad angry at me, but I don't want to lose Ramon either."

"Maybe people here at the hospital who know him can talk to your dad. You know—put in a good word. I mean, Ramon wouldn't be working here if somebody didn't think he had value. Besides, everybody deserves a second chance."

Bonnie was right. By allowing her dad to be judge and jury over Ramon, she had sided with her parents against him. She should have fought harder to keep her friendship with him. She liked him. She wanted to have him in her life. Who knew if such an opportunity would come her way again? Her diseased heart was directing her life already. Why should she let her parents direct it also?

"I'm going home today, before he comes in."

"So see him after you get home."

Laura chewed her bottom lip. "Will you help me?"

"Sure." Bonnie's eyes lit up, as if she would relish the adventure.

"I guess I could get his address somehow, and his phone number."

"Ask that nurse Betsy. Tell her you want to write him a thank-you note."

Laura considered Bonnie's idea. "You have a devious mind." She grinned. "But I do like the way it thinks."

Bonnie bowed with a flourish. "What are friends for?"

Dr. Simon came in while Laura's parents were packing her things up to return home. "It's good to see you up and around, Laura."

"I feel pretty good," she said.

"Sit down," Dr. Simon said. "I want to talk to all of you."

Dread crept over Laura as she and her family settled into chairs and faced the doctor.

"What's up?" Laura's father asked.

"I have the results of your latest tests." The

doctor opened a manila folder. "You've lost ground, Laura. I don't think you can afford another infection. Your heart's just too weak."

Her bluntness startled Laura.

Mrs. Carson took Laura's hand. "So what are you saying?"

Dr. Simon gave the three of them a level but somber look. "I'm going to put you on the beeper."

Six

"**Y**ou're recommending me for a heart transplant?" Laura asked, her heart thudding from a rush of adrenaline.

"Yes. It's your best hope. You know we've discussed it before."

Laura remembered. Her diseased heart would be replaced with a donor heart. When one became available, she would get beeped on a pager that she would always wear. If it happened in the dead of night, she'd get a phone call. She'd have minutes to leave for the hospital, where she'd be prepped for surgery and wheeled into an operating room. Hours later, she would emerge with a new heart sewn into her chest. She had wanted to keep her old heart, the one she'd been born with. She'd hoped that medical science would come up with another solution, but today Dr. Simon had closed that door with the assignment of a beeper. The idea of having her heart cut out and replaced was terrifying.

"There's no other way?" she asked.

Dr. Simon shook her head. "Not anymore."

"Then let's do it," she said, making up her mind in an instant. With a new heart, perhaps she'd be able to truly live again.

"When?" her father asked.

"Unfortunately, it could be a long wait, especially at this particular transplant center. There are many people in need of a heart ahead of you, and usually the sickest people get organs first. Some people actually sell their homes and move to other states to have a better chance of receiving an organ sooner."

Laura absorbed the implications of Dr. Simon's words. Was she suggesting that they move to improve her chances?

"The problem with relocating, however, is that you may trade expertise in the transplant team for the shorter wait." Dr. Simon glanced from face to face, then added, "I just want you to know all the facts."

"What about a match?" Laura's mother asked. "What are the chances that a heart will come along that suits her and no one else?"

"We only match blood type and body size because we don't have time to do much else once a heart becomes available. She'll need a heart that can fit inside her chest. Fortunately, she's achieved her adult height, so a comparable-sized heart should be easier to match. It would have been much harder when she was a child."

"And rejection?" Laura's father asked.

"Laura will have to take antirejection drugs for the rest of her life. But they've improved tremendously over the past few years. Once she heals, she should be able to resume a normal life."

To Laura, it sounded like a dream coming true. How she had longed for a normal life! A new heart would make it possible.

Her father stood and held out his hand. "Thank you, Doctor. You've given us plenty to think about."

Dr. Simon turned to Laura. "Now go home

and stay well. You'll be notified by the transplant center to come in for psychological evaluation. Organs go to people who are properly motivated to take care of themselves. I'd like to see you back here in two weeks for a checkup. If there is any—and I do mean *any*—problem, you call me."

Laura watched her mother complete the packing process, her mind spinning. She was going to have a heart transplant. That is, if she lived long enough for a heart to become available. She wanted to tell Ramon. The hurdle of her parents' objections toward him seemed small to her now. Once she got a new heart, she'd be able to do what she wanted with her life. For the first time in years, Laura Carson felt as if she had a future.

Laura didn't have one second alone before leaving the hospital, so she never got to ask Betsy for Ramon's address. And once she was at home, she was tucked away in her bedroom where her father showed off the computer and Minicam system he'd installed for her.

"All you have to do is rotate this dial, and a camera will pick up in each of your classrooms. See? Here's your English class." He turned the dial, and a black-and-white picture of Mr. Arnold's classroom from a high back corner angle popped into focus on a TV monitor screen on her desk beside her computer. School was over for the day, but come Monday morning at ten, every chair would be filled. "Now you try it," her father said.

Laura flipped the dial, and Ms. Stanton-myer's Algebra II classroom popped onto Laura's home screen. "That's neat, Dad. Not a bad way to go to school."

Laura hoped she sounded more enthusiastic than she felt. Her parents had gone to a lot of trouble and expense for her sake, and she knew she should be appreciative. But all she could think about was Ramon and the way they had parted.

"Each teacher will wear a wireless mike, so you'll be able to hear every word," her father said. "No excuses for zoning out during lectures," he added with a chuckle.

Laura began her electronic classroom attendance. With ambivalent feelings, she watched the kids in her classes moving across the monitor screen. A month before, she'd been a part

of their world. Now she was a watcher, looking at her high school peers unemotionally,
hardly remembering why she'd thought it important to ever return to that place. The difference wasn't in them, but in the fact that she
was going to get a new heart. And that she had
met Ramon.

Three days later, she called Bonnie after
school and said, "I've called the hospital and
asked for Ramon, but I was told that he was an
hourly worker and if it wasn't an emergency,
I'd just have to leave him a message."

"So what's the problem?"

"I've left him two messages, but he hasn't
called me back."

"What do you want to do?"

"I know he works at a grocery store called
Sanchez Market in his neighborhood. I've
found the address online." Laura took a deep
breath. "I want to go look for him. And I want
you to go with me. You said you'd help me
once before."

"And I will. But how?"

"Mom's starting back to work Monday, so
I'll be alone here for six whole hours. We can

go and get back before she gets home. They'll never know."

"I don't know, Laura, it sounds risky. What if you pick up some germ?"

"I'll take the risk. I have to see him, Bonnie. Please . . . won't you help me?"

"Are you sure, girls? That's a pretty mean neighborhood." The cabbie looked at Laura and Bonnie in his rearview mirror.

"We're sure," Laura said.

The ride across town to Spanish Harlem seemed to take forever and used a large chunk of the money Laura had saved up, but they finally pulled up to a crowded sidewalk in front of a small grocery store. A few homeless men sat in nearby doorways asking passersby for money while children played in the street. Laura stepped over an old woman curled up asleep on a grate. Inside, the store had harsh fluorescent lighting and smelled of exotic spices and vegetables. Narrow rows of cases were filled with produce, and the aisles were packed with ethnic foods in colorful boxes and bags.

Bonnie asked, "What if he's not here?"

That thought hadn't occurred to Laura. "He's got to be."

She marched over to a cashier and asked for Ramon. The bored older woman looked her over, then pointed. "He's in the back, scrubbing floors in the walk-in cooler."

Laura walked to the rear of the store, Bonnie dogging her heels. She stopped at the open cooler door. Her heart raced. Ramon's back was to her, and she said, "Hello, Ramon. How are you?"

He turned, his face registering shock. "Laura! What are you doing here? Why have you come?"

"Because you wouldn't answer any of the messages I left," she said, her voice trembling.

"What messages? I got no messages from you. I was told never to contact you again."

Seven

Laura was certain that her parents had issued the order. "I apologize for my parents because they had no right to tell you that," she said. "It's wrong. When I didn't hear from you, I was hurt. I thought maybe you were just tired of me."

Ramon dropped the mop with a clatter, came to her, and held her face between his large, rough hands. "I could never forget you, Laura. Haven't I told you that many times? Seeing you again has made me the happiest I've been in a week."

Her knees turned to mush. Behind her, Bonnie cleared her throat. Laura introduced them.

"Come," Ramon said. "I'll take you some-place away from here."

"That's all right. We don't mind—"

"No," he said sharply. "You aren't safe here."

Laura didn't feel in any danger, especially now that she was with Ramon. "But your job—"

"I don't care." He removed the long apron he was wearing, took her hand, and led her toward the front door. He said something in Spanish to the cashier, then escorted Laura and Bonnie outside and around to the narrow back alley. There he put both girls into a beat-up old car. "It's not much," he said, "but I bought it myself."

He drove past the graffiti-covered buildings down to a park in Midtown, not speaking the whole way. He somehow wedged his car into a tiny parking space. In the park, the trees were bright with new leaves, and tulips bloomed in well-kept flower beds. Mothers and nannies pushed baby carriages along sun-dappled walk-ways. He found an empty bench overlooking a bed of daffodils and settled Laura beside him.

Bonnie said, "I'm hungry and I see a hot dog vendor. Want me to get you both something?"

They shook their heads. Laura realized Bonnie was only giving her and Ramon a chance to be alone, and she was grateful. Because he'd been so quiet, she was afraid she'd really blown it by showing up at his job unannounced. "I—I'm sorry I interrupted you at work," she began.

He wove his fingers through hers and stared deeply into her eyes. "I don't care about the job. It's you I care about. We left because I did not want you in my world, Laura."

"But why?"

"It is an ugly, scary world and not good enough for you."

"That's silly. I wasn't afraid."

He dropped his gaze. "But I am. I still have enemies there."

"Then why do you stay?"

He shrugged. "Sanchez gives me a free room over his store in exchange for watching over his turf at night. I save money more quickly. It is a good arrangement for me."

"I don't want to stop seeing you," Laura blurted out. "I don't care what my parents think."

He turned, stared across the beds of swaying

yellow flowers. Finally, still holding on to her, he said, "The things your father told you about me are all true. I am not a good person. I have done many bad things. Such things I do not want you to know about. Or hear about. I've been in juvie jail. I once led a gang in my neighborhood, where my word was law." He lifted the sleeve of his shirt and she saw the faint tattoo of a dragon. "I'm having this removed by my friend Carlos in the radiation department at the hospital. If only all of my past were so easy to erase."

Laura felt hot and cold all over, but she didn't find his past repulsive. "That's not the Ramon I know. My Ramon is kind and gentle and very caring."

His shoulders sagged. "When I came home from jail, two of my best friends were dead. Also my cousin was dead, and my brother was in custody for shooting a rival gang member. In the past four years, I have lost six friends to the streets. I knew that if I didn't do something for myself, I would end up the same way. That's when I started working at the hospital, trying to make something better of myself. And that's where I first saw you.

"You were so beautiful, so sick and sad. I

could not take my eyes from you. Of course, you did not know I existed. I can't explain why you made a difference for me, but you did. I wanted to know you. I wanted to be worthy of you and your world. You gave me purpose even though you never knew me. Or knew how I felt about you."

She was moved. His feelings for her transcended reason, and she didn't feel worthy of them. Tears formed as she imagined the harshness of his youth, the loss of his friends. "I didn't know, but I'm happy you've told me. My parents had no right to tell you not to ever contact me."

"You are lucky to have such parents. My father left when I was two. My mother struggled to raise us, but she got sick and died. We moved in with an aunt, but my uncle was a drunk and very cruel. The gang world was safer, and in the gang I was somebody important. As I grew, my reputation grew as being one mean *hombre*. By the time I was fifteen, I had a long history with the cops. My uncle became frightened of me. He did not beat me then, but he did turn me in to the cops. And so I was sent to the detention center."

Laura knew she should be frightened by a guy like Ramon. He'd led a life she'd only read about in newspapers. Yet she wasn't afraid of him. Worse, she was certain she was falling in love with him. "I don't know what to say except that all that happened to you before doesn't matter to me. I want to see you again. Especially now."

"You're on the transplant list. *Sí*, I have heard. But that is a good thing, Laura. With a new heart, you can live a long life and not be sick. It makes me happy to know this."

She gave a nervous sigh. "But I'm scared. Scared I'll get the heart; scared I'll die waiting. Either way is a risk."

He nodded. "Life is risk. When you grow up on the streets, every day you don't die is a good day." He smiled shyly. "But I don't want to speak to you of death, but of life. And you have given my life new meaning."

She couldn't believe that he felt so strongly about her. She knew she wasn't extraordinary, but he certainly made her feel as if she were. "Then that's all the more reason why we should plan on seeing more of each other."

"It would mean much to me if we could. But how? Your parents—"

"Want me to be happy," she interrupted. "And being with you makes me happy. I'm under their junkyard dog guard right now, but once they relax, I'll have more freedom. In the meantime, I'll be making regular visits to the hospital. Bonnie will help us get together."

"Did I hear my name?" Bonnie came up with a half-eaten hot dog and a cola. "I—um—don't mean to be a drag, but we'd better get home. It's almost three, and school will be getting out. We both need to be where we're supposed to be."

"I'll drive you," Ramon said, standing. "Then I'll clock in at the hospital."

"And on the way we'll make some plans," Laura said. She wasn't going to let anything separate her from Ramon. Now that she'd found him again, she wasn't going to lose him. No matter what her parents said.

With Bonnie's help, Laura was able to get and receive messages from Ramon regularly. As Laura got stronger, she begged Bonnie to accompany her to the hospital for checkups and visits. "You can call Dr. Simon and yak your heads off," she told her parents. "But please don't hang all over me now that I feel good. I'm not a kid anymore."

Her parents, at first hesitant, finally agreed, and so after every visit, Laura met with Ramon. They took walks by the river, holding hands. When Laura grew short of breath, Ramon would sit with her on the riverbanks. They'd watch the currents and talk about one day being together. She'd never been happier.

Her life felt so almost normal that on some days she forgot she needed a new heart. And her real heart was so full of joy that even Dr. Simon commented on her excellent attitude. "Research shows that the better your outlook, the quicker your recovery," Dr. Simon told her.

And her parents said, "It's wonderful to see you so happy, honey."

Of course, Laura couldn't tell any of them *why* she really felt the way she did—she couldn't tell them about seeing Ramon, but she was glad they'd noticed.

In late July, her father dropped a bombshell.

"Laura," he said one night at the dinner table, "we're closing up the town house here in the city and moving to Mississippi. I've done a lot of research, and it's your best shot at getting a new heart quickly."

Eight

〜

"**B**ut I don't want to move to Mississippi" were the first words out of Laura's mouth.

"Why not? I've looked into this carefully," her father said. "If you stay here, your wait for a heart could be up to four years. In Mississippi, it could be less than eight months."

"And it's not as if we won't return," her mother offered. "Just as soon as the transplant's over and you've recovered, we'll come home. All we're going to do is take up residency in another state so that you'll have a better chance of getting your heart sooner. We'll sublet the town house."

"But what about my doctor? Dr. Simon can't operate in Mississippi." How could her parents consider such a thing just when she was doing so well? Just when she was so happy.

"Dr. Simon has checked out the transplant facility and transplant team in Jackson, and she thinks you'll be in good hands."

"I won't be able to begin my senior year at my high school. I—I was looking forward to school in the fall."

"I think getting a heart is far more important than where you attend high school," her mother said.

"But all my friends are here. There's Bonnie—"

"She'll understand. I don't know what all the fuss is about, Laura. This news should make you glad."

Laura felt her breath catching in her throat. She practiced a relaxing technique she'd learned from the psychologist preparing her for the transplant procedure. "It does," she said slowly. "You just caught me off guard, that's all."

Her father smiled. "Good. Then I'm flying

down this weekend to look for housing. We need to establish our residency as soon as possible."

"What about your business?" Laura tried one last tactic.

"Bill will keep it running." He named his store manager. "I've told him I'll make him a partner."

"You will?"

"There's nothing more important to your mother and me than you. The business is secondary and always will be."

She was out of arguments. Her chest felt caught in a vise, and her mind wouldn't shut off. She would be moving, and there was nothing she could do about it. She *had* to talk to Ramon.

Bonnie set up the meeting, and Laura took a cab to the park on the riverfront that was her and Ramon's favorite meeting place. He was already there, pacing and looking worried. "Are you all right?" he asked the minute he opened the cab door.

"No," she said, a knot of tears wedged in her throat.

Ramon took hold of Laura and walked with her slowly on the path toward the river. She told him about the upcoming move, her heart fluttering, her breath ragged. "What are we going to do, Ramon? I don't want to move."

By now they had reached the river. Ramon spread out the blanket he'd been carrying and made her sit. Taking a bottle of drinking water from his knapsack, he moistened a napkin and dabbed her forehead and neck. "You must not get so upset. It's not good for your heart."

"Aren't we going to talk about this? Do you want me to move?"

He flashed her a dark, hurt look. "Every minute I have with you, Laura, is like a small gift. A present that I don't deserve. I've always known that you would one day leave me."

"But I'm not leaving because I want to," she cried.

"And isn't that the point? You're leaving because getting a new heart is more important than anything else. Even us."

"I—I just thought it would happen here with you nearby."

He took her into his arms and kissed her damp cheeks. "Don't cry. It hurts my heart to see you cry. Do you think I want to see you go? I would be with you every minute if I could."

She settled against his chest, heard the drumming of his heart. It calmed her. Her rapid heartbeat slowed. She imagined returning to him with a new heart. She would be whole and well, without blue nail beds and blue lips. "We'll have to think of a way to talk to each other when I'm living down there. I couldn't stand not talking to you for as long as this may take."

"How long before you move?"

"As soon as Dad can find us a place and movers can be lined up."

Ramon brushed her hair away from her face and smoothed her cheek. "Before you go, I will speak to your family. I've wanted to talk to them for a long time about us because it isn't right to deceive them. I want them to know I love you."

"And I want them to know that I love you," she said, clinging to him.

"Then I will speak to them whenever you can set it up."

She felt better knowing that they would be

able to be open about their feelings for each other. Her parents probably hadn't changed their minds about Ramon, but this time she was determined to stand up for what she wanted. She wanted them to know how badly they'd misjudged Ramon. And she wanted him in her life—he was just the medicine her heart needed to grow strong for the journey ahead of her.

He cupped her face between his hands. Ribbons of bright yellow sunlight lit up his hair and shoulders. His dark brown eyes glowed. "I was saving something to tell you, but I'll tell you now because I can't keep it a secret anymore."

"Tell me."

"I've been accepted into a program to become a medical technician . . . all expenses paid."

She knew how much he wanted a career in medicine and momentarily forgot her own dilemma. "But that's wonderful! When do you start?"

"In September. I'll give up my grocer's job but still work at the hospital. When the course is over, I can start a new job at the hospital. My supervisor has already said so. He recommended me for the program."

She put her arms around him. "I'm happy for you."

His gaze turned tender, and he brushed her cheek with the back of his hand. "I couldn't have done it without you."

"I didn't do anything. You did all the work."

"You gave me hope. You gave me the courage to act on my dream."

Cradled in each other's arms, they watched the river until the sun began to sink behind a stand of trees. Laura felt soft as velvet, as if warm liquid had filled her mind and soul. In Ramon's arms, all her troubles, all her fears faded. She wished she could stop time and hold these minutes like jewels. But she couldn't. The sun began to dip in the west. "I have to go," she said reluctantly. "My parents think I'm at Bonnie's."

"I'll take you there, but first . . ." Ramon reached into the knapsack. "This is for you." He handed her a slim leather book, beautifully embossed in gold.

"Poetry?" she said, reading the cover.

"Love poems. They say what I want to say

with such beautiful words. I do not have such lovely words. But if I did, I would say them all to you."

She smoothed her hand across the binding, her heart full of love for him. "I'll treasure it always."

"Until we can be together forever," he said.

She wrapped her arms around his neck. "Forever," she whispered.

He leaned forward and kissed her with a kiss so achingly sweet that it made her cry.

On the following Monday, Laura's father returned from Mississippi with news that he'd found them a small house in Jackson, not too far from the hospital. Laura knew things would begin to move rapidly now, and the sooner they knew about her and Ramon, the better. She told Ramon to plan to come over on Saturday and that she would handle the rest. She plotted with Bonnie for the best way to break the news. She rehearsed a speech, deciding to tell them on Friday after dinner, but early Friday morning, she was roused from a sound sleep by her mother.

"Get dressed," her mother said.

Laura struggled awake. "Why? What's happened?" Light from the hall spilled into her room, outlining partially packed boxes.

"We just got a call." Her mother's voice trembled with emotion.

Laura hadn't heard the phone ring because at night the ringer on the phone in her room was turned off. Her bedside clock glowed 4:30. "A call?"

"From the hospital. Dr. Simon said to come immediately. They have a heart for you, Laura. They need to operate right away."

Nine

"B-but how?" Laura shook off the stupor of sleep. "The list—"

"I don't know how. They just said to come." Her mother had turned on the light and was quickly packing the small bag Laura always took to the hospital. "Get dressed. Dad's bringing the car around."

Her father drove through the darkened, almost deserted streets like a maniac. At the hospital, a team of doctors and nurses rushed out to meet them. They put Laura into a wheelchair and wheeled her upstairs to be prepped for surgery. She was groggy with pre-meds when Dr. Simon came in, dressed in hospital scrubs.

"How are you doing?"

"All right." Laura's tongue felt heavy. "How . . . did . . . this happen?"

"I'll tell you all about it after the transplant." Dr. Simon took her hand. "Dr. Rodriguez will be the chief surgeon. I'll assist. When you wake up in recovery, you'll have tubes everywhere, including one down your throat, so you won't be able to talk. Once you're stable, we'll move you into ICU. Your parents want to be with you now. I'll see you inside the OR."

Dr. Simon was replaced by Laura's mom and dad. Their faces looked pale and anxious, but they smiled and squeezed her hand. "We'll see you in recovery," her father said.

"We love you, honey," her mother said. "We'll be waiting for you when you wake up. Be strong."

"I love you too," Laura said.

Laura was wheeled into a brightly lit, icy cold operating room, bustling with activity. A doctor with dark brown eyes and a surgical mask in place leaned over her. "I'm Dr. Rodriguez. Are you ready?"

She nodded, all apprehension gone as the

preop medications took effect. "You're Hispanic," she said, her words slurred. "Like Ramon. That's good. Do you know him?"

"No." He patted her shoulder, distracted by another doctor who introduced himself as her anesthesiologist.

"I'm going to slip this mask on you, Laura. You'll be asleep in seconds," that doctor said.

From the corner of her eye, she saw an adjoining operating room door swing open and heard another doctor say, "The patient's ready for retrieval."

She felt a deep sense of pity, then gratitude. In the next room lay her donor.

"We're ready here too," Dr. Simon said.

The mask slid over Laura's mouth and nose. The sounds around her faded, and she tumbled headlong into a river of darkness.

Laura was aware of a bright light spilling into her eyes and a voice calling her name. Her chest felt as if a great weight were pressing her down. She tried to move but couldn't.

"Laura, wake up," the voice said. "It's over, honey. Wake up now."

She struggled to open her eyes and squinted

at the light. "That's the girl," the voice said. "The surgery's over and you're doing fine."

"Honey?" another voice said. "It's Mom and Dad, Laura. Can you see us?"

She saw her parents and a nurse behind them. She couldn't move. Her bed was an island in a sea of high-tech equipment. Tubes seemed to be sprouting from her body. Her throat was completely closed off. She felt immense pressure across her chest, but no pain.

"Look at your nails, Laura." Her mother lifted Laura's hand for examination.

Laura saw that her normally blue nail beds were pink, her fingertips rosy.

"The new heart's working, baby. It's doing a fantastic job already. Oh, Laura, we're so happy." Her mother's quiet, joyful sobs blended with the steady beep of regular, bright green lines displaying the rhythm of her new heart across the screen of her heart monitor.

Laura nodded slightly, then closed her eyes. The transplant ordeal was over, and she was alive!

The tube down her throat was pulled the next day, and she had never been so glad to be rid of anything. She could talk again, but the one question she wanted answered—Where's Ramon?—she couldn't ask. She was kept in a sterile room, and her only visitors were doctors and her parents. All had to wear paper gowns and masks. She was still monitored by an array of equipment, and despite strong pain medication, she hurt. "The worst is over," Dr. Simon told her.

They had her out of bed by day three. She took a few hesitant steps and felt as if she'd run a mile. By the end of the week, she could sit up in bed unaided, and many of the tubes had been removed.

"You're doing fine," Dr. Simon said. "I'm amazed at how quickly you're recovering. It's because you're young, Laura. And because you have an incredible will to survive. Keep up the good work."

"I have questions." Laura's voice was still raspy from the tube.

"I know. And I'll answer all of them. But not now. Not until you're stronger. Not until we're sure you won't reject."

The constant flow of antirejection drugs had made Laura's face round as the moon. She was told it would return to normal when the drugs were backed off, but after looking at herself in the mirror, she was glad Ramon hadn't seen her. Still, she missed him terribly and kept thinking of ways to get him a message. She asked her mother if she could talk to Bonnie on the phone. Perhaps Bonnie could get messages to and from Ramon.

"Um—Bonnie's well aware of what's happening, but she had to go off on vacation with her family. You can call her in another week."

Laura thought it strange. Bonnie hadn't mentioned any vacation plans. And without Bonnie's help, there was no way she could contact Ramon. "When am I getting out of ICU? When am I going home?"

"You'll have to ask Dr. Simon," her mother said, which seemed uncharacteristically vague. Her mother always knew everything.

Laura grew anxious as the days passed with no word from Ramon. She lay awake at night, her mind racing. *Where are you, Ramon? Why haven't you found a way to contact me?*

Laura was twelve days into her recovery when Dr. Simon came in and pulled up a chair beside her bed. Since she'd already checked Laura earlier in the day, Laura hadn't expected her. "Is something wrong?" she asked. "Is my heart all right?"

"You're doing fine. In fact, I'm going to release you very soon. You can complete your recovery at home."

Laura grinned. "That's what I've been waiting to hear."

Still, Dr. Simon didn't move. "There's something else I want to talk to you about. Remember the night of your surgery, when you asked me how you advanced on the list so suddenly?"

"I remember." Laura sat straighter in bed. She'd wondered about that ever since she'd awakened after the transplant. She knew that donors' names were kept confidential, with a recipient meeting a donor's family only rarely and under special circumstances. "We were planning to move, you know."

"I know, and moving was your best bet until this happened." Dr. Simon held a manila folder on her lap. "One way to move up on the recipient list is to have a donor designate an organ to a recipient. It's done all the time in kidney transplants. A relative will agree to give a kidney to another relative so that person can go directly into surgery without having the long wait for a cadaver kidney. The odds of rejection are lower too, because many of the genetic factors are similar."

"What's that got to do with me?"

"I'm going to show you something." Dr. Simon opened the folder and removed a newspaper clipping. "It's not going to be an easy thing for you to see, but you must." She handed Laura the clipping.

It was written in Spanish, so Laura couldn't really read it. But she didn't have to. There was a photo of a body lying on a sidewalk. Two words jumped off the page at her: *Ramon Ochoa*.

Ten

"No," Laura cried, burying her face in her hands. "No. No. No."

"I'm sorry, Laura. So very, very sorry." Dr. Simon held her close and let her weep.

When she was able, Laura asked, "H-how did it happen?"

"It was a drive-by shooting. Ramon was working late at his second job—some grocery store in Spanish Harlem. He was sweeping the sidewalk out front. Witnesses said a car full of Hispanic males drove past and opened fire. He was hit in the head. Paramedics gave him CPR and transported him to our ER. The police think the shooting was gang related."

"But Ramon wasn't in a gang. Not anymore."

"I'm only telling you what's suspected."

"Did they catch them?"

"The police are still looking."

Laura felt sick to her stomach and thought she might vomit. Leaning back against her pillows, she shut her eyes.

"I can get you a tranquilizer," Dr. Simon said.

Laura shook her head. She didn't want to be groggy. A pill would only dull the pain, and she didn't want the pain dulled. She ached for Ramon, for herself. For all that was lost.

"I think Ramon had a premonition that his life would end badly."

"What do you mean?"

"He came to see me months ago. He said he wanted to be an organ donor, but there was a stipulation. He said if anything happened to him, he wanted his heart to go to you. He told me he didn't care about the rest of his body just as long as you received his heart."

Laura moaned. The heart beating inside her was Ramon's. How could she have not known? How could she have not sensed his presence?

"I tested him that afternoon. You have the same blood type. That made it a real possibility for him to be your donor."

"He never told me. *You* never told me."

"He didn't want me to, and I couldn't— doctor-patient confidentiality. Besides, I never dreamed it would happen. But he was insistent and told me to make it legal. We made out a living will on the spot, and I promised him I'd follow his wishes. He carried a card in his wallet with my name on it and instructions to call me first if anything happened to him. When he was brought into the ER, he had massive brain damage. There was nothing that could be done to save him. We got him onto a ventilator and called you. For what it's worth, his organs saved five other people that night."

Still numb with shock, Laura thought about her parents' objections to Ramon. "Do my parents know?"

"Yes, I've told them. And they're very grateful to him. They're setting up an educational fund here at the hospital for minorities to take medical courses like Ramon wanted to do. It's generous of them."

"They should have told me."

"I wouldn't let them. I wanted you to be stronger when you heard. We knew it was going to be difficult for you. We all want you to live."

"Why? Ramon's gone." Laura couldn't stop trembling.

"Don't talk that way. He wouldn't want you to give up."

Laura turned her face toward the wall. She felt desolate. Her reason for getting well was gone. Without Ramon, how could she go on?

"He loved you, Laura. He told me that when I asked him why he'd will his heart to you."

Still Laura said nothing.

"He gave me this to give to you. But only if anything happened to him." Dr. Simon removed a long white envelope from the folder. "I'm going to go now, so you can read it in private." She laid the envelope on Laura's lap and walked to the door. There she turned and said, "Ramon Ochoa gave you the greatest gift one human being can give to another—he gave you life. Don't let go of it. Make his gift count."

Laura stared at her name neatly printed across the front of the envelope. Her hands shook as she opened the flap and pulled out a piece of paper. Through a blur of tears, she read:

Mi Cara—*My dearest Laura,*

If you are reading this, then I am gone and you have my heart inside you. That was my greatest wish, and Dr. Simon promised she would help fulfill it.

I don't know how my life ended. Perhaps I was crossing a street and was hit by a car. Yet I do not think that is how it really happened. As I told you, I have lived most of my life by the rules of the streets. And people like the person I used to be have long memories. They hold on to grudges because they have nothing else to hold on to. Two years ago, it was said to me, "No one leaves the Dragons, Ramon." Getting out was a dream, but dreams rarely come true in my part of the world.

I'm sure you must be surprised to know that I have given my heart to you. But what else could I do? Knowing you, loving you was the bright light of my life. Knowing that you loved me was what gave me life. So it seems right that my heart should rest with you in death as it did in life.

Please, do not cry for me. I have peace now. I have a place on the river outside of time, and there I will wait for you. And when you come, even if you are an old woman, I will know you. For I will recognize my heart within you.

Take care of it. Grow old. And come to me when the angels call your name.

Te Amo (I love you),

Ramon

P.S. I gave you a book of poems once. They said things more lovely than I could ever say them. I liked the poem on page 37 best. Read it and think of me saying those same words to you.

Laura was crying so hard that it was difficult to breathe. She pressed the paper to her cheek, knowing that his hands had touched it, written it, folded it. She watched the heart monitor beside her bed reflecting the steady pace of her heart, half expecting the line to break and shatter from the weight of her sadness.

Ramon's heart was now Laura's heart, melded into her body by a surgeon's skill, and it was sustaining her. He had wanted her to live, and Laura knew then that she would. Living was her price to pay for the privilege of holding his heart for safekeeping. Life was the mandate he'd given her on the night he died by assassins' bullets. She would not, could not, let him down.

Despite her haste to get to the hospital on the night she was called for her transplant, she had taken the time to tuck her poetry book into her suitcase. Now she took it from the bedside table drawer where she'd asked one of the nurses to put it days before. It had been her one link to Ramon during her hospital stay, and she loved touching it and tracing his signature with her finger. She'd read all the poems but quickly turned to the one he'd named as his favorite. Her breath caught.

She read the poem slowly, tasting the words, savoring each one, imagining Ramon whispering them to her. By the time she reached the final lines, she was crying so hard she could barely see them. But it wasn't necessary. She knew them perfectly. The words were stamped into the fabric of her mind, the tapestry of her heart. They were:

> "—*I love thee with the breath,*
> *Smiles, tears, of all my life!—and, if*
>   *God choose,*
> *I shall but love thee better after death.*"